P.A.M.

Written by:

Ed Wise

wiseed@hotmail.com
859-835-8456

EXT. LAKELAND HIGH SCHOOL - DAY

2020s architecture, but worn. Students roam. No cars or other
era related objects are visible.

INT. LAKELAND HIGH - HALLWAY

Crowded with students. In the background is a banner that
reads, "Come to the Twentieth-Century Dance".

EUGENE, 16, a scrawny nerd, weaves through the crowd, catches
up to, then walks alongside, CANDICE WALKER, 16, chewing gum.

                    EUGENE
          Going to chess club?

                    CANDICE
          Probably.

Candice stops at a locker. Eugene grins, then invades her
space.

                    EUGENE
          Got a new opening move, bet I beat
          you.

Eugene's eye's bulge in fear as he sees something behind
Candice, then he slinks away.

                    CANDICE
              (under her breath)
          First time for everything.

In the background, JACK CLAWSON, 17, a bully, intercepts
Eugene, then tosses him against a locker.

Eugene struggles to hold his arm up. On his forearm is a slap
band-like phone.

INSERT: PHONE SCREEN

A bank logo and "Transfer $50.00, To: Jack Clawson". Eugene's
finger taps "Send".

BACK TO SCENE

Clawson smiles, then releases Eugene, who races away.

Candice, seeing this, shakes her head

JOCK, 18, big, and in a varsity jacket, goes to the locker adjacent to Candice, then opens it.

                         JOCK
          Someone should help Eugene.

Candice nods. Jock grabs something from his locker then leaves. Candice chews her gum, pops a bubble, then watches Clawson and his cronies push their way through the crowd.

                         CANDICE
              Someone will.

Candice opens her locker and sees...

INSIDE CANDICE'S LOCKER

Paraphernalia of a school girl and a small box in a corner. A hologram projects from the box as the locker door opens. In the holo, Young Candice finishes a piano concerto.

INTERCUT CONCERT HALL STAGE/WING - NIGHT - CONTINUOUS

Young Candice stands, turns to the packed music hall then bows. The spectators erupt in applause. Young Candice motions to a wing for someone to join her.

In the wing, BILL WALKER, aka "Pops", 40s, geeky, and PATTY WALKER, 40s, in new, but poor quality formal wear, (aka their formal clothes) stand teary eyed and proud. Bill holds a bouquet of roses.

A stage manager nudges Bill and Patty onto the stage. They nervously join Candice who receives the roses. Bill and Patty flank Candice, hold hands, then the three bow as one.

INT. LAKELAND HIGH - HALLWAY

Candice smiles, kisses her finger tips, then taps the hologram of them.

                         FENG (O.S.)
              Most girls have holos of boy bands
              in their lockers.

Candice smiles, closes the locker, then turns to FENG, 17.

                         CANDICE
              I'm not most girls.

Candice melts into the crowd. Feng follows her.

                    FENG
          True.

Feng struggles to keep up as Candice wends her way through
the throng.

                    FENG (CONT'D)
          Got a date for the dance?

                    CANDICE
          No.

                    FENG
          Want one?

Candice stops, then turns to Feng.

                    CANDICE
          What about Skyler?

                    FENG
          We had a fight.

Candice nods, then starts walking again. Feng rushes to catch
up. Candice glances over her shoulder at Feng as she walks.

                    CANDICE
          And that made you decide to switch
          teams?

Feng blushes, then becomes nervous.

                    FENG
          Not exactly.

Candice stops, then glares at Feng.

                    CANDICE
          We're supposed to be friends. Why
          can't you be honest with me?

                    FENG
          Whatdaya mean?

                    CANDICE
          You want me to go to the dance with
          you to make Skyler jealous. But you
          don't want to make him too jealous
          by going with a dude.

Candice starts walking again. Feng stands embarrassed and
bewildered, then yells after her.

                         FENG
                    Well, will you?

Candice vanishes into the crowd. Feng stands frustrated. A
phone BEEPs. On Feng's arm phone, a text from Candice reads
"Yes, but apologize and ask Skyler first".

INT. GRUNGY RESTROOM - DAY

A small truck-stop-like restroom.

LENORE WAGER, 40s, in coveralls, takes off some nitrile
gloves while wrapping them in a small pair of scissors, then
puts the wad in her pocket.

As she's washing her hands, Lenore practices faces in the
mirror. First happy and waving, then shocked and fearful. She
dries her hands, then leaves.

EXT. SMALL AIRPORT - CONTINUOUS

A prop plane with a large open cargo door idles by a hanger.
A sign in the background reads, "Bowman Sky Diving". Lenore
walks out in helmet, goggles, and parachute, then climbs in
the plane.

INT. PLANE - IN FLIGHT - CONTINUOUS

Lenore sits next to husband, 50s, who's scared. She turns to
him and grins devilishly.

                        LENORE
              Relax honey, try and enjoy yourself
              going down.

Husband grins and nods nervously. Lenore enters the doorway,
then jumps out.

EXT. SKY DIVE - CONTINUOUS

Lenore is in free fall.

                        LENORE
                 Good luck with that.

Lenore pulls a baseball sized object from her pocket, tosses
it in the air, then pulls a cord to release her parachute.
Lenore zips "up" and out of the frame as the parachute opens.

In the background, a videodrone unfolds from the "baseball" Lenore had thrown. This is a cross between a "GoPro" camera and a quadcopter drone.

Lenore floats back into the frame. The drone zips over to her and videos her as she floats down.

Lenore pulls cords, turns, and waves at the drone. It moves in and out from her as it catches various angles.

Lenore mimics the faces she'd practiced in the restroom. She smiles and waves as the videodrone follows her through the sky.

In the background, Husband zips by with his parachute flailing above him.

Lenore's face morphs into fear and shock. She turns away from the videodrone, looks down at husband, then gives him a finger wave.

                    LENORE (CONT'D)
          Ba bye.

EXT. WALKER HOME - DAWN

The sun peeks over the horizon on a middle class suburban two-story home. Somewhat futuristic, but not overly so.

INT. WALKER HOME - GARAGE

The sound of a toy train O.S. Twentieth century movie posters related to trains dominate a wall.

Cheap bookcases line the other walls. These contain a movie collection comprised of reels, VHS, DVD, and BluRays. Train memorabilia is mixed in.

This includes four binders titled "Dunkirk Model 7000 Hypertrain, BUILD SPECIFICATIONS, Volumes A, B, C, D.".

A model train layout fills the center of the garage. Several trains of different eras (steam, diesel, and bullet), run through country and city settings.

Bill, in a conductor's uniform and hat, gleefully works controls.

                    PATTY (O.S.)
          Bill, can I speak to you?

Bill turns at her voice and his arm hits a bullet train that derails.

                    BILL
          Darn it.

Bill puts the train back on the track, then walks into...

INT. WALKER HOME - DINING AREA - CONTINUOUS

Silent and dimly lit.

Patty sits at a table looking at a hologram of a receipt from "Thrifty Mart". To the side of it, two numbers are circled, "$212.68", and "$52.16".

Bill creeps up behind Patty, then kisses the top of her head.

                    BILL
          Mornin' hon.

Bill goes to a coffee pot, pours a cup for himself, brings the pot back, then tops Patty off. Patty points at the hologram.

                    PATTY
          Notice anything unusual about these
          numbers?

Bill, confused, sets the pot down, then sips his coffee.

                    BILL
          One's bigger than the other?

                    PATTY
          Right. One's a lot bigger than the
          other. One is how much you spent on
          the cake, the other is how much I
          would have spent making it.

Bill sighs.

                    BILL
          The store bought ones are so much
          better.

Patty glares at Bill.

                    PATTY
          So much better than who's cake?

> BILL
> Umm, ahh, yours, ahh, nobody's...
> Sorry, I'll buy the mix next time.

> PATTY
> Bill, honey, just get what I put on
> the list. I could've had the whole
> order delivered for less than the
> difference in the cake.

> BILL
> Gottcha... How're we doing anyway?

Patty moves some files around in the holo.

A bar chart labeled "Total Assets", shows a steeply upward
trend of bars. A dotted line is near the top and reads
"Amount Needed for PAM". The final bar exceeds the PAM line.

Patty sits back and smiles. Bill, confused, looks at the
holo.

> BILL (CONT'D)
> Is that good?

> PATTY
> Yes Bill, that's good. We're ahead
> of target. Unless the market tanks,
> we'll have enough to get her
> through college.

> BILL
> You're a genius hon. I don't know
> where I'd be without you.

> PATTY
> Now all we need is to get her
> accepted.

Bill opens the refrigerator.

INSIDE THE REFRIGERATOR

A cake with a piano in the icing, and "Happy Birthday, Paris,
Here I Come!".

Bill's finger moves towards the cake.

> PATTY (O.S.)
> Don't even think about it.

Bill's hand jerks from the cake, then grabs a lunch box.

INT. WALKER HOME - DINING AREA - CONTINUOUS

Bill kisses Patty, then moves to leave.

                    BILL
          Slam dunk. No one plays like
          Candice.

EXT. RED ZONE - NIGHT

Rainy and gloomy. A sparsely populated urban slum. Nefarious
activities abound; drug deals, solicitation, etc.

Candice, with an umbrella and chewing her gum, walks down a
street. She passes storefronts with barred windows and doors.
A few street people look at her and nod.

WILLY, a thug with a club in hand, jumps from the shadows.

                    WILLY
          Hey baby, got something for me?

Candice moves her umbrella, sees Willy, then pops a gum
bubble.

                    CANDICE
          Hey Willy.

Willy, surprised, relaxes.

                    WILLY
          Hey Candice.

                    CANDICE
          Kinda busy and it's--

                    WILLY
          I know, raining.

Candice nods, then walks past Willy.

                    WILLY (CONT'D)
          Ahh, Candice...

Candice turns to Willy.

                    WILLY (CONT'D)
          Do me one. Don't tell Mrs. Cho
          about this? She doesn't like--

                    CANDICE
          Yeah, I know. Anyone pulling shit
          on her block... Except her, of
          course.

                    WILLY
          Right, yeah. Thanks.

Candice walks in front of a black building. The glass in the
former windows has been removed and the spaces are bricked.
The door is solid steel with no handle.

Candice walks confidently towards the door. There's a BUZZ
AND A CLICK, then the door opens automatically.

INT. SECURITY SHOP - CONTINUOUS

A row of glass cabinets are filled with hand guns, grenades,
knives, etc. The wall behind it is covered with machine guns,
a futuristic bazooka, gun laden drones, etc.

A sign reads, "If you don't see it, ask for it. We either got
it, or can get it". Another reads, "Just In, Facial
Recognition Proximity Mines".

MRS. CHO, 40s with a jewelers loop on and behind the counter,
holds an electrical probe that goes into a compartment of a
futuristic machine gun.

A Goon, in body armor and camo gear, watches her.

                    CHO
          Targeting C. P. U.'s shot.

Goon looks at Cho questioningly.

                    CHO (CONT'D)
          Scrap metal.

The front door opens automatically. Goon looks nervously at
it. Candice, drenched, strolls in, then folds her umbrella.

                    CHO (CONT'D)
          Hey Candice.

Candice pops a bubble then waves politely at Cho.

                    CANDICE
          Hey Mrs. Cho.

Goon stares at Candice as she confidently walks towards a
heavy metal door in the rear of the store. There's a BUZZ AND
A CLICK.

The door opens by itself. Candice strolls in. The door
closes.

Goon looks at Cho curiously. Cho grins in return.

                    CHO
          A friend of my son.

Cho lifts up the heavy gun, then looks down the barrel.

                    CHO (CONT'D)
          I can give you twenty thousand. Not
          a penny more.

INT. SECURITY SHOP - BACK ROOM - CONTINUOUS

Cluttered with boxes. Feng plays a holographic video game.
Candice walks in, then grabs a towel.

                    CANDICE
          Clawson's number's up.

                    FENG
          I figured. You need something from
          up front?

                    CANDICE
          No. Pops says violence should be
          the last resort.

Feng pauses the game, then looks at Candice curiously.

                    FENG
          Now you're quoting Pops?

                    CANDICE
          First time he's said anything that
          made sense... I think I'll try
          letting Clawson know he should be
          more careful with his secret.

                    FENG
          Secret. What secret?

                    CANDICE
          Dunno. But everyone's got one.

Feng snickers.

                    FENG
          Where'd you get that one? Family
          movie night?

Candice nods.

                    FENG (CONT'D)
          I thought you slept through those?

INT. LAKELAND HIGH - CLASSROOM - NIGHT

A clock reads "8:32 p.m.".

BENNY BOOKTA, 50s, wanders around observing students playing
chess. Some congratulate each other, then leave chatting.

Candice and Eugene remain, Bookta moves to, then looms over
them. Candice moves a piece.

                    CANDICE
          Check mate.

Eugene, pissed, knocks over his king, then rushes towards the
door. Candice yells after him.

                    CANDICE (CONT'D)
          Maybe you need another new opening
          move?

Eugene flips off Candice as he exits. Bookta sits.

                    BOOKTA
          Ever think of letting him win?

                    CANDICE
          You told me to never do that. That
          life wasn't fair and we had to work
          twice as hard as anyone else to get
          what we deserve.

                    BOOKTA
          So I did. Any word from PAM?

Candice gets up, then packs personal things.

                    CANDICE
          REE-Jected.

                    BOOKTA
          Seriously? Have you told your
          parents?

Candice, teary eyed, shakes her head.

                    CANDICE
          Not yet. I'm afraid they'd both
          stroke out and I'd be orphaned.

Bookta nods.

> BOOKTA
> What's next?

> CANDICE
> That's it I guess.

> BOOKTA
> Your Pops teach you to quit this
> easily?

Candice, pissed, glares at Bookta.

> CANDICE
> Hypothetically speaking, would a
> student get in trouble for telling
> a teacher to mind his own damn
> business and go screw himself?

> BOOKTA
> Have it your way. Just sayin.

> CANDICE
> Pops is loaded with clichés two
> hundred years old. Crap like "don't
> jump to conclusions" and "don't
> judge a book by it's cover".

Candice continues packing her things.

> BOOKTA
> Maybe it's too early to conclude
> that you're not going to PAM. It
> ain't over 'til it's over.

> CANDICE
> Damn Mr. Bookta, not you too.

Candice puts on her backpack, then sighs.

> CANDICE (CONT'D)
> I get it. I guess I'll just have to
> work three times as hard.

Bookta shakes his head in frustration as he watches Candice
leave. The door closes, then Bookta, pissed, lifts his arm
phone.

> BOOKTA
> Call Maddie.

INTERCUT MADELINE IN HER BEDROOM/BOOKTA IN THE CLASSROOM

The bedroom has a French motif.

On the walls are pictures of MADELINE ST. CHARLES, 50s, aka "Maddie", and dignitaries shaking hands in high profile locations such as the oval office, Kremlin, and Forbidden City.

All of the pictures have Madeline, various adults, and a different teenager with a musical instrument.

Madeline is in bed with a sleeping mask on. An arm-phone lays flat on a nightstand.

                    MADELINE'S PHONE
          Incoming call - Benny.

Madeline sits, slides the mask up, glances at a clock, and sees, "2:43 a.m.".

                    MADELINE
          Shit... Answer.

A small hologram of Benny in the classroom materializes.

                    MADELINE (CONT'D)
          Do you know what time it is in
          Paris?

Bookta shakes his head.

                    BOOKTA
          Don't care... You said she was in.

                    MADELINE
          She was.

Madeline, in a tee and pajama bottoms, gets up, then "slaps" the phone around her forearm.

                    MADELINE (CONT'D)
          (mumbling to herself)
          Screw it, might as well go in.

Bookta cleans up the classroom, puts chess sets away, cleans up food wrappers, soda cans etc., throughout the scene.

                    BOOKTA
          And?

Madeline slips on bunny slippers with huge ears, then walks towards a doorway. She snaps her fingers at a coffee maker as she walks, then coffee starts to brew.

                         MADELINE (O.S.)
                    Now she's out.

Madeline walks through a doorway.

In the classroom, Bookta sits, then becomes serious.

                         BOOKTA
                    Maddie, I'm not asking for a favor.

In the bedroom, there's the SOUND OF PEEING O.S., THEN A
TOILET FLUSHES O.S.

Madeline comes back in, sits at a vanity, then brushes her
hair.

                         MADELINE (O.S.)
                    Good. We promised to never mix
                    business with pleasure.

                         BOOKTA
                    This kid deserves to be in PAM.
                    She's got more talent and works
                    harder than anyone I've ever seen.

A drone carries Madeline a steaming coffee cup.

                         MADELINE
                    Hear it every day. Sorry.

                         BOOKTA
                    What happened? Some billionaire's
                    kid wake up yesterday and decide he
                    wanted to learn the drums so he
                    could be a rock star?

Madeline puts on make-up.

                         MADELINE
                    Senator, guitar.

                         BOOKTA
                    When I had your job I didn't bend
                    the rules.

Madeline puts on a business shirt and tie.

                         MADELINE
                    Yes, you did. Just not as much as I
                    have to now... Look, Benny, we both
                    want to get as many kids educated
                    in music as we can. To do that, I
                    have to pacify a lot of big
                    ego's...
                         (MORE)

                    MADELINE (CONT'D)
          We need coin to fund operations,
          political influence to keep us
          going.

Madeline gets up, then goes into...

INT. MADELINE'S CONDO - HALL

Madeline enters. She's dressed professionally waist up, still
in her pajama bottoms and bunny slippers waist down. A small
holo of Bookta moves a pace in front of her.

                    BOOKTA
          I hate your world.

On the wall is a wedding photo of Madeline and Bookta, as
well as several others of them and a boy at various ages,
including as a teenager with a cello.

                    MADELINE
          It's the same world as yours. I'm
          just on the front lines. You
          decided to quit the fight.

Bookta is surprised and becomes hurt.

Madeline walks into...

INTERCUT BOOKTA IN THE CLASS ROOM/MADELINE IN HER "PAM"
OFFICE

Madeline sits at a plush desk. In the background is an ornate
banner that reads, "Paris Academy of Music", "A Compilation
of the World's Finest Musical Institutions", "Formed 2051".

A dual clock reads, "Paris, 2:48 a.m., Atlanta, 8:48 p.m."

A futuristic skyline of Atlanta is in a clear sliding glass
door. In it is a stadium with a baseball game in progress. A
scoreboard reads, "Atlanta Braves 8, Miami Swordfish 3, Sixth
Inning".

                    MADELINE
          Sorry, you didn't deserve that.
          You've done a lot of good for a lot
          of kids.

Madeline taps the sliding glass door, then the view morphs
into a live feed of Paris, including the Eiffel Tower and
late night tourists.

                    BOOKTA
          Did you watch her Met concert?

                    MADELINE
          No. I had her in on the endless
          testimonials and references you
          wrangled out of everyone we know...
          By the way, how'd you get Philpot?
          He hates everyone.

                    BOOKTA
          Not Candice... Watch it.

                    MADELINE
          You don't get it. It doesn't
          matter.

                    BOOKTA
          It should... Plea...

                    MADELINE
          Don't go there. Your kids get
          treated like everyone else's...
          Well almost everyone else's.

                    BOOKTA
             Sorry.

Madeline sits, then puts on glasses. She appears completely
professional waist up, pajamas and bunny slippers waist down.
She rolls behind the desk and looks at a holographic computer
screen.

On it is a banner that reads "Paris Academy of Music".
Madeline's finger touches an adjacent pad. It glows red then
flashes green.

The holo screen flashes "LOG-IN COMPLETE", then changes to a
huge list of messages.

                    MADELINE
          Look, I'll give her parents a call.
          I've got her on the stand-by list.
          The Senator's kid may decide she'd
          rather be a NASCAR driver.

                    BOOKTA
          Thanks... How're our Braves doing?

                    MADELINE
          Up eight-three in the sixth... Love
          you.

                    BOOKTA
          Love you, too.

Side by side, Bookta, nods, flips a light switch, then leaves
the classroom. Madeline sips coffee and scrolls through
messages.

INT. DUNKIRK TERMINAL - DAY

A futuristic hypertrain station ala Grand Central Station.
Bullet trains are blended into a 1930s French setting.
Bistros and shops are between tracks.

Busy. Some of the "people", (and pets), are androids with
green eyes. They vary from scuffed up animated manikins with
painted on clothing and features, to being life like.

POMPADOUR, 60s, plump and wearing a fedora with a feather,
walks by. A green-eyed robotic lap dog, aka "King" or "King
Edward", is in her purse.

Bill, happily whistling, in his conductor's uniform, with his
lunch box, stops, tips his hat, then goes to pet King.

                    BILL
          My, Mrs. Pompadour, don't you look
          exceptional today. How's King?

                    POMPADOUR
          King Edward is fine. Thank you for
          asking.

King nips at Bill's hand. Bill jerks it back, then smiles.

                    BILL
          He looks like he's being a good
          boy. Do you mind if he has a treat?

                    POMPADOUR
          Certainly Bill, you're too kind.

Bill pulls a fake dog treat from his pocket, drops it from a
safe distance to King, who swallows it whole, then wags his
tail.

                    POMPADOUR (CONT'D)
          The hand soap was running low in
          the ladies room yesterday. I don't
          like to see it less than half full.

Bill attentively looks at Pompadour.

                    POMPADOUR (CONT'D)
          What if several people have an
          emergency at once? Can you be sure
          that doesn't happen again?

                    BILL
          Certainly ma'am, I apologize for
          your inconvenience... Let me get
          you on your way.

Bill goes to the front of the train. A door on it is painted
with "Operator's Cab", the door opens as Bill approaches.

INT./EXT. HYPERTRAIN - OPERATOR'S CAB

Inside is a huge wrap-around windshield. Underneath it is a
large status screen. There are no controls for human
operation. Bill gets in.

                    VIRTUAL ASSISTANT (O.S.)
          Initiating departure sequence...
          Closing doors.

Several lights flash on the status screen, then the door
closes.

Outside, at the track crossing in front, walkways over the
track retract, barriers come down, and flashing red lights
start.

Inside, Bill sits facing away from the windshield.

                    BILL
          Where was I?

Bill raises a circuit board to eye level and frowns.

                    VIRTUAL ASSISTANT (O.S.)
          Passengers secure. All systems are
          within operating tolerances...
          Departing.

On a table in front of Bill is a pile of computer parts.
Behind Bill, a light on the status screen turns green.

Outside, the train slowly pulls out.

Inside, Bill fiddles with a part.

                    VIRTUAL ASSISTANT (O.S.) (CONT'D)
          Reed.

                    BILL
          Admit.

A door in the back of the "operator's" cab labeled "Passenger
Compartments", opens.

REED, 30s, a green-eyed android, taller/thinner than Bill, in
a porter's uniform, enters.

Bill, frustrated, looks at the pile of parts.

In the background, the scenery in the windshield blurs as the
train gains speed.

                    BILL (CONT'D)
          I can't find the clock.

A box labeled "Build Your Own Apple II Replica" sits on a
chair at the table. Reed pulls a circuit board from the box,
then hands it to Bill.

                    REED
          It's this one, sir.

                    BILL
          A board? I thought it'd look
          like... Well a clock. Or maybe
          something related to the period.

                    REED
          A disco ball with hands perhaps?

Bill chuckles as he inspects the board.

                    BILL
          Yeah, right. So, how's the computer
          tell time with it?

                    REED
          It doesn't. It uses it to control
          the rate it does its calculations.

Bill tosses the board back in the box.

                    BILL
          I may need some help with this.

                    REED
          Certainly, sir.

Bill leans back and smiles.

                    BILL
          I've got good news. You're going to
          be freed... Well eventually.

                    REED
          Freed, sir?

                    BILL
          Yup. Patty... That's my wife.

                    REED
          I've had the pleasure.

                    BILL
          The pleasure of what?

                    REED
          Of meeting your wife.

                    BILL
          Right. She likes you by the way...
          Anyway, Patty said Dunkirk wants to
          reduce their capitals and shift it
          to leasing operations.

Reed stands confused, then nods knowingly.

                    BILL (CONT'D)
          The short of it is Patty and I are
          going to buy you, then rent you
          back to Dunkirk. We'll make a
          fortune... Well a lot anyway.

                    REED
          You mentioned freedom, sir.

                    BILL
          Right. That's the best part. Patty
          said that we won't need the rent
          money after Candice graduates from
          PAM... I had to put my foot down,
          but she finally said it'd be okay
          if we freed you then.

Reed, in thought, grins.

                    REED
          Freedom... Hmmm... What does it
          feel like, sir?

Bill snickers.

                    BILL
          To be a droid? I don't know, you
          tell me.

                    REED
          To be free, sir.

                    BILL
          Oh, right. It's wonderful. You get
          to do whatever you want, and enjoy
          life. Truly enjoy it... At least
          when you're not working.

Reed smiles, looks up in thought, then turns back to Bill.

                    REED
          I'll look forward to it, sir.

                    BILL
          Freedom wasn't always free. Why
          back in the day, people had to
          fight for it. It comes with a lot
          of responsibility. You--

                    REED
          Excuse me sir, but how did you come
          by your freedom?

                    BILL
          Well... I... I guess I was born
          free.

Reed nods.

                    REED
          Sorry sir, time for my rounds.

Reed turns, then exits through the "Passenger Compartment"
door.

EXT. POMPADOUR'S HOME - DAY

Palatial with gorgeous manicured rolling hills, statues,
fountains, etc.

A bar overlooks an infinity pool. Pompadour, in a one piece
swim suit and floppy hat, sips a drink by the bar as she
holds King.

CONSUELO, 40s, Hispanic, in nurse scrubs, gives Pompadour a
pedicure and foot massage. Pompadour jerks her foot back.

                    POMPADOUR
          Ouch. They're feet, not some frog
          you're dissecting in high school.

King barks and nips at Consuelo.

                    CONSUELO
          I'm sorry ma'am.

Pompadour pets King, then glances at Consuelo.

                    POMPADOUR
               (dismissively)
          Like you ever went to high school.

                    CONSUELO
          Excuse me, ma'am, I was a doctor in
          Haiti.

                    POMPADOUR
          And now you're an illegal in
          Atlanta that does pedicures... Go
          figure.

MAID, African American, in a French maid outfit, exits the
distant house, then walks towards Pompadour. Pompadour points
at her.

                    POMPADOUR (CONT'D)
          I could turn your ass in to ICE and
          replace you with one of her kind.

As Maid nears, it's clear that she's a green-eyed android.

                    MAID
          Miss Lenore.

Lenore, in sunglasses, and dressed to the nines, strolls in.
Pompadour shoos Consuelo away.

                    POMPADOUR
          Dismissed. Wait in your spot.

In the distance, next to the pool, in the bright sun, an "X"
is on the pool's apron. Consuelo goes to it, then stands.

Lenore plops down in a lounge chair next to Pompadour, snaps
her fingers, then points at the bar. Maid fixes a drink.

                    POMPADOUR (CONT'D)
          When will the estate settle?

                    LENORE
          His kids accepted our offer last
          night, we should get the coin
          within a month.

                    POMPADOUR
          Good. It costs a lot to keep this
          place going.

Lenore looks around.

                    LENORE
          Maybe we should cut back a bit?

                    POMPADOUR
          No. We need to maintain this image
          if you're going to land the right
          husbands.

                    LENORE
          Actually there's a problem with
          that. Bernard says--

                    POMPADOUR
          He's the marriage planner?

Maid delivers the drink. Lenore takes a pull.

                    LENORE
          Yes, Momma.

                    POMPADOUR
          When I was your age we didn't need
          someone to figure out how to get a
          guy to marry us. We just found the
          richest one we could, then screwed
          his brains out until he begged us.

                    LENORE
          Blah, blah. I know... Back when
          hamburgers were a nickle... Things
          are different now.

                    POMPADOUR
          Doubtful. I think people are
          screwing exactly the same as they
          were thirty years ago.

                    LENORE
          Everyone does background checks.
          Bernard says I've gotten a
          reputation for being a gold digger
          who only marries executives that
          don't live long.
                    (MORE)

                    LENORE (CONT'D)
          He can't figure out how to get
          anyone with more than half a brain
          to marry me.

                    POMPADOUR
          Damn.

                    LENORE
          Right, damn. He says I may have to
          marry a dumb ass.

                    POMPADOUR
          Hmm. Not many of those that are
          rich. It's going to be hard to find
          someone.

                    LENORE
          Boo, hoo. You wanna trade places?

Pompadour sucks in her stomach, then admires her plump
physique.

                    POMPADOUR
          Don't temp me, I could still pull
          it off.

Lenore stands, does a twirl, then admires herself.

                    LENORE
          Maybe we should have a Joe six-pack
          lottery. The winner gets to sleep
          with me.

Pompadour grimaces.

                    POMPADOUR
          Gross. I've done that before. I was
          drunk, but not black-out drunk so
          I'd forgotten it in the morning...
          Better get yourself a full body
          condom and a shit load of booze.

Lenore grins, then lays back in the lounger.

                    LENORE
          The sacrifices I make for you.

                    POMPADOUR
          So you have to marry a moron for a
          while. I slept with your step-
          father for ten years before I
          whacked him.

                    LENORE
          If you would've done it at eight he
          wouldn't have been raping me for
          two years.

Lenore waves at Consuelo who's watching from the distance,
then snaps her fingers.

Consuelo wipes sweat from her brow, frowns, then walks to
Lenore.

                    POMPADOUR
          If you would've told me, I would
          have. Anyway, like him, it's water
          under a bridge... I'll try and find
          you a better one this time.

Lenore nods as Consuelo approaches. Lenore slides off her
heels, and exposes gross feet. Consuelo looks inquisitively
at Lenore, glances at her feet, then grimaces discretely.

                    LENORE
          Easy on the bunions.

INT. WALKER HOME - CANDICE'S BEDROOM - NIGHT

Neat. Piano memorabilia dominates. A clock reads "2:53 am".
Wide eyed, Candice lays in bed with covers pulled up to her
nose.

Candice's slap-band phone lays flat on a night stand. It
lights up.

                    CANDICE'S PHONE
          Get outta bed you sleepy head.

Candice gets out of bed, gets on her hands/knees, then crawls
to...

INT. WALKER HOME - UPSTAIRS HALL

Candice slithers down the floor, reaches the stairway, then
peers down into...

INT. WALKER HOME - LIVING AREA

Bill stands in front of the sofa, Patty sits on it. Both are
in their "formal clothes", now worn.

                    BILL
          How could they not accept her?

Patty shakes her head.

                    PATTY
          We'll get it straightened out.

Bill practices a speech.

                    BILL
          Good morning, Ms. Saint Charles.
          How's the weather in Paris?

                    PATTY
          Bill, honey, maybe you should let
          me handle this.

                    BILL
          No, no. I got it. I just need to
          practice a bit.

Bill straightens himself.

                    BILL (CONT'D)
          Good morning. Did you get the
          recording we sent?.. No. Damn-it.

A holo of Madeline at her desk at "PAM" forms behind Bill.

                    MADELINE
          Hello, is anyone there? Behind you,
          Mr. Walker.

Bill pales, then turns to face holo Madeline. Like a deer in
headlights, he stares slack jawed and frozen in fear.

INTERCUT LIVING AREA/MADELINE AT PAM/CANDICE AT THE STAIRS

Madeline, anxiously taps a pen, looks at a monitor, sees
"Appointments" and a list that fills the screen.

                    MADELINE
          Perhaps I should call another time?

At the top of the stairs, Candice peers down, sees Bill, then
mouths "you can do it Pops".

Bill sees her, then animates.

                    BILL
          No this is fine... Ms. St. Charles.

Madeline sighs.

                    MADELINE
          Call me Madeline... Mr. Walker, as
          you're well aware, PAM is the
          world's finest musical academy. We
          only accept the most exemplary
          candidates. Unfortunately, Carmine
          just missed our criteria.

                    BILL
          Candice.

                    MADELINE
          Right, Candice. Unfortunately,
          we've filled our quota for the next
          freshman class. While unlikely,
          it's possible that some may chose
          not to attend. In that case--

                    BILL
          But Candice is amazing. She's had
          her second concerto at the Met. Did
          you receive the tape we sent?

At the top of the stairs, Candice looks on and edges closer.

Madeline taps her computer screen, then a list of mail pops
up.

                    MADELINE
          Yes, yes, I have it here somewhere.
          I don't agree that she's amazing...
          Very good possibly.

Bill stares into the holo of Madeline.

                    BILL
          Very good? No, Candice is
          exceptional. She's worked very
          hard. Isn't there something that
          can be done?

                    MADELINE
          I'm sorry, Mr. Walker. Good--

Madeline reaches towards her phone. A red icon on it reads
"End Call".

Candice's eyes shoot open. She rushes down the stairs, then
shoves Bill out of the way. He plops down on the sofa next to
Patty. Hands on hips, Candice stands glaring at holo
Madeline.

Madeline, taken aback, sits with her finger over "End Call".

                    CANDICE
              (evil then softening)
          Don't you do it! You didn't even
          watch the holo! I know I'm not
          perfect, but I've dreamt of going
          to PAM since I was a child.

A tear forms in Candice's eye.

                    CANDICE (CONT'D)
          Won't you listen? Just five
          minutes. If I'm no good, we promise
          to never bother you again. Please?

Bill and Patty sit holding hands and anxiously look on.
Candice stands visually pleading.

                    MADELINE
          Well, you're certainly tenacious.
          Hmmm... Alright, I'll give you five
          minutes, no more.

Madeline glances at a clock.

                    MADELINE (CONT'D)
          Go.

Candice quickly sits at the piano in the corner then begins
Rachmaninoff's second concerto. Her fingers alternate from
gently caressing the keys to pounding them.

Madeline stares blankly, then her eyes move to photos on her
desk. In them are Madeline, Bookta, and the boy with a cello.
She resignedly shakes her head, then turns to Candice.

                    MADELINE (CONT'D)
          Okay, okay, that's enough.

                    CANDICE
          Please, I beg you, accept me to
          PAM, I'll do anything.

                    MADELINE
          A little rough, but not bad. You
          present yourself well and relay
          your emotion through the
          keyboard... I assume you have the
          resources for her to attend? I'll
          need a deposit in five days.

Bill nods sheepishly, then turns to Patty, who stands.

                    PATTY
          Not a problem.

Madeline turns to Candice.

                    MADELINE
          Congratulations. Welcome to PAM.

Madeline makes some notations.

                    MADELINE (CONT'D)
          You'll be starting in fall seventy-
          four's freshman class. We'll see
          you in two years.

INT. WALKER HOME - LIVING AREA - CONTINUOUS

Holo Madeline fades. Candice stands elated. Patty hugs her.

                    PATTY
          Congratulations, honey.

                    BILL
          Did we do it?

INT. MADELINE'S CONDO - PAM OFFICE - CONTINUOUS

A holo of the Walker living area fades. Madeline gets up,
waist down she's in her pajamas and bunny slippers. She
slides open the door with the Paris skyline then walks
onto...

EXT. MADELINE'S CONDO - DECK - CONTINUOUS

Bookta stands smoking a cigarette and watches a baseball game
in the adjacent stadium. Madeline walks out.

                    MADELINE
          She's very good.

Bookta takes a drag, then quirks an eyebrow at Madeline. She
sighs in return.

                    MADELINE (CONT'D)
          Okay. Exceptional.

Madeline takes the cigarette, then puffs it. They continue
exchanging the cigarette as they speak.

                    BOOKTA
          Remind you of anyone?

                    MADELINE
          She's exactly like him.

                    BOOKTA
          I know, right.

                    MADELINE
          Those eyes. First a darkness. Like
          she wanted to jump through the holo
          and rip my head off. Then so sweet.
          Like the cutest puppy I ever saw. I
          wanted to hug her.

                    BOOKTA
          None of us are what we seem... You
          put her in?

Madeline nods.

                    MADELINE
          Those idiots piss me off. I mean, I
          know what they're thinking. It's
          just one more student, you've got
          twenty thousand. What's one more?
          Stick her in a corner. But we're
          absolutely full. If an entitled kid
          comes in, a deserving one goes out.

                    BOOKTA
          So you ditched the Senator's kid?

                    MADELINE
          Yeah, she'll have to learn to
          drive.

Madeline locks eyes with Bookta.

                    MADELINE (CONT'D)
          You know I'll probably get fired
          for this.

Bookta nods, then moves to hug her.

                    BOOKTA
          I know. I did, remember... I'm
          proud of you for making a stand.

                    MADELINE
          Even a futile one?

                    BOOKTA
          Even a futile one.

INT. WALKER HOME - LIVING AREA - EVENING

A bowl of popcorn is on a coffee table. Candice in sweats, lounges on a sofa and watches a holo of a movie ala "Star Wars".

Arm in arm, Patty and Bill walk down the stairs and into the living area. Both are in their worn formal outfits. Patty's fitting perfectly, Bill's is tight in the middle.

Candice stands and admires them.

                    CANDICE
          Wow Moms, you look awesome. And
          Pops you look...

Bill sucks in his stomach.

                    BILL
          I know, I could lose a few pounds.

                    CANDICE
          Right Pops, a few.

Bill holds Patty's hand up, then she does a twirl.

                    CANDICE (CONT'D)
          Still got it Moms.

Patty looks at Candice's attire, then frowns.

                    PATTY
          Why don't you put on something
          nicer? It's a dance, you might meet
          someone.

                    CANDICE
          I don't want to meet "someone". I
          know what I want and it's not a
          human being. At least for now.

                    PATTY
          I'm just worried about you honey. A
          little balance would be good.

                    CANDICE
          Between piano and keeping you two
          out of trouble, I've got enough
          balance.

Bill grabs Patty's hand, then leads her towards the door.

                    BILL
          Come on we're going to be late.

                    CANDICE
          Have fun.

                    BILL
          You too. Be home by one.

Patty and Bill head for the front door. Candice grabs Bill's
arm, taps a record icon on his phone, then smiles at Bill.

                    CANDICE
          So I can watch when you get home.

Candice pecks them on their cheeks, then melts into the sofa.

                    CANDICE (CONT'D)
          Remember to leave the fob for the
          car.

Bill stops, flustered, he turns.

                    BILL
          I thought Feng would pick you up.

                    CANDICE
          He would, but this way I can leave
          as soon as he and Skyler get back
          together.

Bill reddens. Candice stuffs popcorn in her mouth.

                    BILL
          Actually, we're going to be using
          the car.

Candice leaps up.

                    CANDICE
          No Pops, we talked about this.
          You're going through the red zone.

                    BILL
          We'll only be in it a few miles...
          Do you know what a secure cab
          costs?

Candice lifts her arm phone.

                    CANDICE
          No, Pops, they don't know you
          there. I'm ordering you a cab.

Bill rushes Patty out, then turns as he closes the door.

                         BILL
                  We'll be fine.

Worried, Candice puts a piece of gum in her mouth and starts
chewing furiously. Then she pulls a side curtain back and
peers out to see...

EXT. WALKER HOME - DRIVEWAY

Bill and Patty approach a worn, but clean, four door sedan
(aka Bill's car) parked in the driveway.

The car's symmetrical with no apparent front or rear. No
headlights/taillights, side view mirrors, or controls for
human operation.

A holographic chauffeur appears and makes movements to open a
door. The holo is glitchy, and the movements out of sync with
the door movement. Bill and Patty get in. Then the car drives
off.

INT. WALKER HOME - CONTINUOUS

Candice stands peering out the window, then shakes her head.

                       CANDICE
            I wish you'd listen to me, Pops.

EXT. GREEN ZONE - DUSK

A busy street. The cross walks are clearly painted, but there
are no traffic lines for cars, or traffic signage.

Self-driven cars and trucks move efficiently around. Some
have opaque windows. In the ones that can be seen in, the
front seats are backwards, with occupants facing each other.

On the sidewalk, in the background, is a sign meant for
pedestrian traffic, "Red Zone, 1000 feet" and an arrow.
Bill's car goes towards the red zone.

INT./EXT. BILL'S CAR - CONTINUOUS

Inside are four seats facing each other. A small table is
between them. There's no driver or controls. Bill and Patty
sit in the rear seats holding hands. Bill smiles at Patty.

                         BILL
                  Champagne?

Bill pulls out a bottle of champagne. Patty jerks the bottle
from Bill, then inspects the label.

INSERT: THE BOTTLE'S LABEL

"Suzie's Champagne, Bottled with Love in Boise, Idaho" and
"may contain artificial flavor, color, and carbonation".

BACK TO SCENE

Patty grins, then Bill takes the bottle back.

                    BILL
          It's in our budget.

                    PATTY
          Keep it that way.

                    BILL
          Can't we loosen things up a bit?
          Candice is in, we have the coin.

                    PATTY
          No. The do-do always hits the fan
          when you least expect it.

                    BILL
          It'll be fine.

Bill undoes the wire strap on the cork. Patty sees this, then
dives for cover under the table.

INT. PATTY UNDER THE TABLE - CONTINUOUS

Patty sees worn carpet, hears the cork "POP" and it
RICOCHETING around.

The cork comes to rest near Patty's face, then champagne
drips from the table to the floor. Patty sighs, then sits up.

INT./EXT. BILL'S CAR - CONTINUOUS

Bill sits with two champagne flutes, then hands Patty one.

                    BILL
          To the last twenty years and the
          next twenty to come.

Patty smiles, accepts the glass, then takes a sip.

                    PATTY
          Will you tell me where we're going
          now?

Bill smiles ear to ear.

                    BILL
          Bistrot Dubois.

The car passes happy people pushing strollers and jogging.

                    PATTY
          Bill, we can't afford that.

                    BILL
          I know. But Candice told me if I
          didn't take you, she'd botch her
          next concerto on purpose so we
          wouldn't need to save anymore.

Outside the car, in the distance, a gate is in a tall wall
with coiled barbed wire atop. A green-eyed guard with two
green-eyed pit bulls stand vigilant.

Bill looks out a window, see's the gate, then grimaces.

                    BILL (CONT'D)
          Privacy.

The car's windows turn opaque.

Inside, Patty shakes her head.

                    PATTY
          She'd do it, too.

                    BILL
          I know. What was I supposed to do?

                    PATTY
          I don't suppose we could get fast
          food and lie to her.

                    BILL
          She said she was going to check the
          chip as soon as we got home. Plus
          there's this.

Bill shows Patty his arm phone, a "record" icon is lit on it.

                    PATTY
          Can't get anything past that girl.

Bill's car, with opaque windows, nears the gate. A sign reads, "SECURE TRANSPORT IS RECOMMENDED IN THE RED ZONE". Another reads "Danger level 8.9/10.0"

The gate opens, then the car drives through.

Inside, Patty snuggles into Bill, then he puts his arm around her.

Outside the car, hordes of destitute people mill about. Tents cover the sidewalk and encroach the street.

Four THUGS, 20s, inked and in black leather jackets, warm their hands over a flaming barrel.

Bill's car, with opaque windows, slowly weaves around obstacles, (burned cars, tents, shopping carts, etc.).

Thug 1 turns to Thug 2, nods towards Bill's car, then smiles.

> THUG 1
> Pay day.

Thug 2, curiously turns, see's Bill's car, then nods in return.

In the car, Bill takes Patty's glass, sets it down, then admires her.

> BILL
> You're as beautiful as the day I
> met you.

Patty smiles. Bill moves to kiss her. Patty's eyes close, her mouth readies.

Outside, the four thugs move to the car. Thug 2 jumps directly in front of it. Bill's car stops abruptly. It nudges and jerks towards Thug 2, but doesn't hit him.

Bill pulls back from the kiss.

> BILL'S CAR
> Warning, forward path obstructed.

> BILL
> Clear windows.

The windows clear. Thug 2 stands directly in front of the car. Thug 1 taps a piece of pipe on Bill's window.

> THUG 1
> Give us what we want and you'll be
> home by midnight.

Thug 1 looks past Bill to Patty, grins, then licks his lips.

                    THUG 1 (CONT'D)
          She won't be back 'til morning
          though.

Bill's eyes widen in fear.

                    BILL
          Reverse.

The car goes backwards. Thug 3 steps behind it. The car
stops.

                    BILL'S CAR
          Warning, rearward path obstructed.

Bill looks outside the car and sees the four thugs with an
array of weapons. Bill's jaw drops, then he goes into shock
and freezes. Patty nudges him.

                    PATTY
          Bill what are we going to do?

Patty nudges Bill again. He's frozen in fear.

                    PATTY (CONT'D)
               (authoritatively)
          Call for help.

                    BILL'S CAR
          Dialing nine-one-one...

The Thugs begin to strip the car. Poles are used to pry up
the corners and blocks are set to remove the tires. Thug 1
smiles in the window.

                    THUG 1
          Take your time. I've got all night.

*Director's note: The voice of the 911 operator should sound
synthesized/pre-recorded. Specific words/times patched in.*

                    911 OPERATOR (O.S.)
          You've reached the emergency
          response department of... Advanced
          Police Services... By calling this
          number you agree to indemnify and
          hold us harmless from any...

Thugs remove tires. Bill is in shock. Patty is confident, but
slowly losing it.

                    911 OPERATOR (O.S.) (CONT'D)
          Damages occurring as a result of
          any response we may undertake.
          Please disconnect if you don't
          consent.

Patty shakes her head, then polishes off a glass of
champagne.

                    PATTY
          Damn-it

                    911 OPERATOR (O.S.)
          Please refrain from using
          profanity... What is the nature of
          your emergency?

Patty shakes her head in frustration.

                    BILL
          My husband and I are near the
          corner of Oak and Second...

A thug walks away rolling a tire at his side.

                    911 OPERATOR (O.S.)
          I'm aware of your location...
          Madam.

Patty becomes more upset.

                    PATTY
          Several thugs are attacking us.

                    911 OPERATOR (O.S)
          It's inappropriate to characterize
          people as... Thugs... unless you've
          received their permission.

A thug slides under the car, then starts undoing bolts. Patty
takes a pull from the champagne bottle. Bill sits in shock.

                    911 OPERATOR (O.S.) (CONT'D)
          A squad car will be dispatched. The
          estimated response time for your
          location, Third and Locust, is...
          four hours and... twelve minutes.
          Please be patient.

A battery pack drops from Bill's car. Two thugs drag it away.

Patty, scared and teary eyed, looks at Bill.

                    PATTY
          Do something! Candice needs us.

Bill shakes himself out of it, then glances out the window.

Outside, Thug 1 taps on it with his pipe, then give's Bill a
devilish grin.

                    THUG 1
          We need to wrap this up, it's
          almost my bedtime.

Thug 1 winds up to smash Bill's window.

Bill takes a deep breath.

Thug 1 smashes the window, reaches in, then grabs Bill.

                    BILL
          Emergency code nine-nine-three.
          Critical infra-structure contractor
          in distress, request immediate
          assistance.

Thug 1, in fear, loosens his grip, then locks eyes with Bill.

                    THUG 1
          What the... Who are you?

Thug 1 looks skyward curiously.

                    911 OPERATOR (O.S.)
          You have been identified as... A
          Hypertrain Engineer... for Dunkirk
          Transportation.

Thug 1 let's go of Bill, turns, then runs. The other thugs
see him, drop the battery pack, then scatter themselves.

                    911 OPERATOR (O.S.) (CONT'D)
          A. R. Forty-seven drones have been
          dispatched. The estimated response
          time is... six seconds.

EXT. SKY ABOVE RED ZONE - NIGHT

Dark, cloudy, with a smogged-over full moon.

A pack of four quadcopter drones hover in formation. They're
twenty-five feet in diameter. A box with a gun barrel is on
the base underneath them.

On a side is, "A/R-47 Drone", a hatch reads ".45 Caliber Ammunition ONLY".

The drones race down single file.

EXT. DRONE ATTACK STREET LEVEL - CONTINUOUS

The A/R-47 drones split up and track the thugs individually. Machine gun fire erupts from the drones. One by one, the thugs are shredded with bullets.

Bill's car is blocked up and tireless, wires dangle from below. Bill peers from the broken window, then takes a pull from the champagne bottle.

An aerial view summarizes the destruction.

All four Thugs are dead with mutilated bodies. Several other corpses are scattered. Nearby buildings are ablaze and a dirty CHILD with a raggedy doll wanders aimlessly crying.

                    CHILD
          Mommy?

INT./EXT. BILL'S CAR - CONTINUOUS

Bill looks out the window, then shakes his head.

                    BILL
          Damn that was close. We'll be okay
          now honey.

Bill turns towards Patty. A flash of moonlight streams through a bullet hole in the car's ceiling as he turns. Patty, in shock, holds her chest. Bill sits confused.

Blood spreads from under Patty's hand and oozes from a corner of her mouth. Bill, wide eyed, reaches down and cradles her head.

                    BILL (CONT'D)
          Oh, Patty.

A small quadcopter with a camera hovers down to the window.

                    CAMERA DRONE
          An aerobulance with M.D. has been
          dispatched.

Bill strokes Patty's hair.

                    BILL
          Help's coming.

Patty, dying, and struggling to speak, pulls Bill closer.

                    PATTY
          Promise me you'll remarry.

Bill pulls back, then looks at Patty in surprise and
confusion.

                    BILL
          What?.. You're not going anywhere.
          You're going to be fine.

Patty pulls Bill closer.

                    PATTY
          Promise me. Promise me you'll
          remarry and do whatever it takes to
          get Candice through PAM.

                    BILL
          Patty, my love, there will never be
          another woman for me.

Patty, blood running from her mouth, grins knowingly and
nods.

                    PATTY
          I know... Marry someone who can
          help you refine Candice.

Bill's tears strengthen.

                    BILL
          Don't leave me Patty.

Patty's nearing death.

                    PATTY
          She needs to know how to handle
          herself with those rich kids at
          PAM... You need to find someone to
          teach her... Promise me.

Wide eyed, Patty dies. Bill weeps, then closes her eyes. The
camera drone hovers in the window.

                    CAMERA DRONE
          We're sorry for your loss. Please
          remember your indemnification to...
          Advanced Police Services.

EXT. LAKELAND HIGH - NIGHT

"I'M GOING TO PARTY LIKE IT'S 1999" BLASTS. A banner reads, "It's the Twentieth-Century Dance". Students, in a wide variety of 20th-century garb, go in a bank of open doors.

INT. LAKELAND HIGH - HALLWAY - CONTINUOUS

A teenaged couple dressed as Bill and Hillary Clinton walk past. Feng and another boy make out in a corner.

Candice peers around her open locker at Clawson, who approaches a locker which has used gum on it. Clawson picks it off, then smells it.

                    CLAWSON
          Fucking Juicy Fruit... Again.

Clawson looks around. The other students avert their eyes.

                    CLAWSON (CONT'D)
          One more piece of gum and I start
          kicking ass until someone talks.

Clawson opens the locker. Inside, stuck against the back wall, is a six inch square box. "Prankster Blaster" is stenciled on it.

                    CLAWSON (CONT'D)
          What the...

There's an EXPLOSION. Clawson is covered in green goo and chicken feathers. The other students laugh and point at him.

Clawson's smoke-filled locker starts to clear. Lettering appears, "Find a new school or everyone learns your secret".

Candice closes her locker, revealing Bookta, dressed as "Elton John", standing solemnly.

                    CANDICE
          It wasn't me.

                    BOOKTA
          Good to know.

Bookta saddens and a tear forms.

                    BOOKTA (CONT'D)
          We need to talk.

Bookta puts his hand on Candice's shoulder, then leads her to a classroom.

                    CANDICE
          Damn. That never ends well.

Bookta, sad and solemn, reaches for the door knob. Candice
stares at him, her eyes widen in fear as she realizes the
news to come.

                    CANDICE (CONT'D)
          Shit... Who?

Bookta opens the door, Candice enters, then Bookta follows.

INT. HYPERTRAIN - OPERATOR'S CAB - DAY

Bill, teary eyed, wearing a black arm band with his uniform,
sits at his table facing backwards. In the windshield, the
image shows the train pulling out and gaining speed.

Bill taps his arm phone.

A holo of Patty and Bill walking downstairs before they left
for Bistrot Dubois materializes. Holo Patty does her twirl.

Bill lovingly tries to touch Patty in the holo.

                    BILL
          Oh, Patty.

                    VIRTUAL ASSISTANT (O.S.)
          Reed.

Bill taps his phone and the holo vanishes. Bill wipes his
eyes.

                    BILL
          Admit.

The door to the passenger compartments opens. Reed, also with
a black arm band, steps in, then remorsefully looks at Bill.

                    REED
          I'm sorry for your loss, sir.

Bill looks curiously at Reed.

                    BILL
          You actually seem like you care.

                    REED
          I do. The last A.I. upgrade you
          authorized has given me the ability
          to be emphatic with human grief...
          Thank you for that.

                    BILL
          Well deserved. These new programs
          seem to have changed you. How do
          you... What's the right word?

                    REED
          Feel, sir?

                    BILL
          Yeah that's it.

                    REED
          I'm experiencing unexpected
          difficulty. I use a sophisticated
          Gantt chart-like sub-routine to
          determine actions. Each coder has a
          style and hierarchy, and their
          priorities differ. I find myself
          confused when two programs lead to
          different outcomes.

                    BILL
          They're called decisions. It may be
          the hardest part of being free.
          Making tough decisions. Especially
          those that involve self-sacrifice
          for the benefit of others.

                    REED
          Why would one ever do that, sir?

                    BILL
          Do what?

                    REED
          Do something that wouldn't be
          beneficial to themself.

Bill nods at Reed.

                    BILL
          I'm afraid you're not quite there
          yet. Maybe with the next upgrade.

Reed stands confused.

                    REED
          Whatever you say, sir.

Bill nods towards the rear of the train.

                    BILL
          How are things back there?

                    REED.
          All systems are within operating
          tolerances.

                    BILL
          Our favorite passenger?

                    REED
          Mrs. Pompadour was napping with
          King when I last checked.

Bill nods.

                    VIRTUAL ASSISTANT (O.S.)
          Engineer Walker, Mrs. Pompadour, in
          first class compartment D, requests
          your immediate attention.

Bill shakes his head,.

                    BILL
          Not napping anymore.

                    REED
          Would you like for me to tend her?

                    BILL
          I doubt she'd let you.

                    REED
          Perhaps not, but I can try.

                    BILL
          Would you?

Reed nods then turns to exit.

                    BILL (CONT'D)
          Ah, Reed.

Reed stops, then looks at Bill inquisitively.

                    BILL (CONT'D)
          You're a good friend.

Reed smiles.

                    REED
          Thank you, sir.

Reed leaves. Bill taps his phone, then Patty's holo
reappears.

INT. LAKELAND HIGH - HALLWAY - EVENING

Deserted and dimly lit. There are several doors with half-glass windows. All are dark, except one. A wall clock reads "6:39". A PIANO PLAYS A FUNERAL DIRGE faintly O.S.

The room with the light on darkens, then it's door opens. Bookta, with a brief case, rushes out from it.

                    BOOKTA'S PHONE
          Incoming call - Maddie.

Bookta grimaces as he rushes down the hall.

                    BOOKTA
          Answer.

A small holo of an angry Madeline forms in front of Bookta as he runs down the hall.

                    MADELINE
          You're late!

                    BOOKTA
          Be there in ten. End.

The holo of Madeline fades. Bookta rushes towards a bank of doors with an "EXIT" sign above. The DIRGE MISSES A BEAT.

                    CANDICE (O.S.)
          Damn it.

Bookta stops abruptly, then shakes his head.

                    BOOKTA
          Shit.

Bookta goes towards a door. The DIRGE GETS LOUDER as he approaches. He opens the door, then steps into...

INT. LAKELAND HIGH - BAND ROOM

The light comes on as Bookta enters.

Well worn musical instruments are scattered, a piano is in the rear.

Candice, alone, teary eyed, wearing a black arm band, is at the piano playing the dirge. Bookta creeps up behind her. Candice stops playing, wipes her eyes, then turns to him.

                    CANDICE
          It's my fault.

                    BOOKTA
          I don't see how it could possibly
          be your fault.

                    CANDICE
          I should've ordered secure
          transport myself.

Candice turns back and resumes playing.

                    BOOKTA
          Your Pops is an adult.

                    CANDICE
          In age only.

Bookta grins.

                    BOOKTA
          You about ready to call it a day?

                    CANDICE
          In a while. Pops asked me to play
          something at the memorial.

                    BOOKTA
          You planning on playing that?

Candice nods as she continues playing.

                    BOOKTA (CONT'D)
          That her favorite kind of music?

Candice stops abruptly, turns to, then glares at Bookta.

                    CANDICE
          She wasn't on anti-depressants.

Candice turns back, then resumes playing.

                    BOOKTA
          What did she like?

Candice SLIPS IN A FEW BARS OF RAG TIME MUSIC INTO HER DIRGE.
Bookta smiles, fumbles around in his briefcase, pulls out
some sheet music, then puts it on the piano.

                    BOOKTA (CONT'D)
          Ever heard this?

Candice grins and STARTS PLAYING "THE ENTERTAINER".

                    CANDICE
          She loved that one.

                    BOOKTA
          Maybe you should play that?

Candice nods and plays energetically.

                    CANDICE
          Thanks Mr. Bookta, you're the best.

Bookta moves to the door, then turns to Candice.

                    BOOKTA
          Jack Clawson transferred.

Candice plays more enthusiastically.

                    CANDICE
          Do tell.

                    BOOKTA
          The only place that would take him
          was a military school.

The pace of the music quickens.

                    CANDICE
          Must've been anxious to leave.

Bookta eyes a pack of "Juicy Fruit" on the piano.

                    BOOKTA
          Thanks Candice.

Candice stops playing, then turns to Bookta.

                    CANDICE
          Pops and I were watching a show on
          how hyenas prey on zebras. The
          zebra's defended themselves by
          staying together as a group.

Bookta looks on curiously.

                    CANDICE (CONT'D)
          He said sometimes we don't have the
          strength to fight a bully by
          ourselves. But if we stick
          together, and look out for each
          other, bully's can't hurt us.

Candice STARTS PLAYING "THE ENTERTAINER" again.

                    CANDICE (CONT'D)
          It was the stupidest thing I ever
          heard when he said it. Funny,
          right?

Bookta nods, then leaves.

INT. LAKELAND HIGH - HALLWAY - CONTINUOUS

Bookta looks in the door window to the band room and smiles.

                    BOOKTA'S PHONE
          Incoming holo-call - Maddie.

Bookta grimaces.

                    BOOKTA
          Answer.

Bookta rushes towards the exit doors. A holo of Madeline
appears and moves in front of him as he races for the doors.

                    MADELINE
          You'd better get your ass here on
          the double. Mother is...

EXT. RAILROAD TRACKS - DAY

Barren train tracks. A hypertrain zips by.

INT. HYPERTRAIN - FIRST CLASS PASSENGER CAR

Reed, in his black arm band, goes to a bank of compartments
then stops. A plate reads "COMPARTMENT D". Reed knocks.

                    POMPADOUR (O.S.)
          Come.

INT. HYPERTRAIN - POMPADOUR'S COMPARTMENT - CONTINUOUS

Pompadour, fuming, and King, barking, sit in plush seats. Two
empty drinks and steak dinners ala a five-star restaurant are
on a table.

Pompadour's meal is a pile of bones, mashed potato, and
asparagus debris. King's meal is untouched. Pieces of
cheesecake are behind each.

Reed enters. Pompadour glares at his black arm band.

                    POMPADOUR
          What's with the band?

                    REED
          There's been a death in the family,
          madam.

Pompadour snickers.

                    POMPADOUR
          One of your toaster off-spring?

Reed politely smiles.

                    REED
          How can I help you Ma'am?

Pompadour looks around.

                    POMPADOUR
          Where's Walker?

                    REED
          He's been detained.

                    POMPADOUR
          By the police, no doubt.

                    REED
          How can I help you Mrs. Pompadour?

Pompadour sighs.

                    POMPADOUR
          Oh, I suppose you'll have to do.

Pompadour points at the food.

                    POMPADOUR (CONT'D)
          These were grossly under cooked.
          I'll not pay for either.

                    REED
          Of course not, Madam. I'll refund
          them to your account.

Pompadour reaches into her purse, pulls out a chip, holds it
out, then nods at the empty drinks.

                    POMPADOUR
          How about comping us a couple of
          drinks?

Reed accepts the chip, sticks it in his neck, then hands it back to Pompadour.

                    REED
          Certainly, madam.

Pompadour points at his arm band.

                    POMPADOUR
          What gives? Who croaked?

Pompadour puts the chip back in her purse. Reed sighs, then composes himself.

                    REED
          Mrs. Walker... If you'll excuse me.

Reed leaves. Pompadour picks up King, who licks her face.

                    POMPADOUR
          Did you hear that snookum's? That
          ghastly Walker creature lost his
          wife.

Pompadour taps on her phone. A holo of Bill pops up and rotates. Pompadour taps an icon on the phone.

Adjacent to Bill's holo, a menu appears, "Human Image Recognition Database", with several icons below. A finger taps "Financial Summary".

Pompadour pets King, glances over the dog, see's a holographic "Net Worth" with a dollar sign and a string of obstructed numbers. Pompadour smiles profusely, then sets King down.

                    POMPADOUR (CONT'D)
          It appears that Walker isn't so
          ghastly after all.

Pompadour taps an icon.

                    POMPADOUR'S PHONE
          Initiating detailed investigation.

Pompadour picks up a piece of cheesecake, then eyes it longingly.

                    POMPADOUR'S PHONE (CONT'D)
          Analysis complete.

Pompadour licks her lips as she holds the cheesecake.

                    POMPADOUR
               Present data.

Pompadour stuffs a chunk of cheesecake in her mouth then eats
voraciously. In the holo, a progression of data/photo's of
Bill's life from childhood race by.

                    POMPADOUR (CONT'D)
               Hmmm. That's good... Oh you didn't,
               you bad boy. Yum, yum.

The data/photo's fly by. Pompadour jams more cheesecake in.

The holo shows Bill, Patty, and Candice being a loving
family. Bill proposing, Bill/Patty's wedding, a robot
delivering an infant to Patty, etc.

Pompadour grimaces, pulls something from her mouth, then
wipes it on a napkin.

                    POMPADOUR (CONT'D)
               Yuck.

Pompadour grabs the other piece of cheesecake and takes a
large bite. The holo shows unintelligible text race by.

                    POMPADOUR (CONT'D)
               That's yummy... Oh yeah... United
               Tech, shoulda bought that myself.

More cheesecake, more data.

                    POMPADOUR (CONT'D)
               Tasty.. You were a genius honey.
               Yum... Why were you with him?

Pompadour absorbs the final bite/byte, swallows, BURPS
loudly, chuckles, then shakes her head.

                    POMPADOUR (CONT'D)
               True love. What a putz.

Pompadour glances out the window, nods in thought, then turns
back. Her face is covered in cheesecake goo. She picks up
King, holds the dog to her face, then King licks it clean.

                    POMPADOUR (CONT'D)
               Call Lenore.

A small iconic hologram of Lenore appears in the remnants of
Pompadour's steak meal. It rotates and flashes as if Lenore
is dancing in the debris of bones, fat, and mashed potatoes.

INTERCUT POMPADOUR/LENORE

Lenore lounges at a spa. Towels are wrapped around her body and head. Two cucumber slices are on her eyes.

                    LENORE'S PHONE
          Incoming call - Momma.

                    LENORE
          Answer... Kinda busy Momma.

A small holo of Pompadour forms in front of Lenore.

                    POMPADOUR
          I see that.

A drone flies a drink with a straw to Lenore, then slides it into her hand. Lenore smiles, sits up a tad, then takes a sip.

                    POMPADOUR (CONT'D)
          Have that marriage planner guy
          check out Bill Walker. See if he
          can figure out how to get him to
          marry you.

Lenore tosses the cucumber slices, then stands. The towel wrapped around her body drops. Lorna does a twirl.

                    LENORE
          How about this plan?

                    POMPADOUR
          We need a little more this time.
          His wife just bit it. The moron was
          seriously in love with her.

Lenore puts the towel back on, then lounges.

                    LENORE
          How much has he got?

                    POMPADOUR
          Enough to be worth our time.

Lenore grabs some cucumber slices from a plate.

                    LENORE
          I'll get Bernard on it.

EXT. SIDEWALK NEAR WALKER HOME - AFTERNOON

Candice and Feng walk side by side.

                    CANDICE
          What did Pops get me?

                    FENG
          Dunno. He just said to be sure you
          were home at six.

                    CANDICE
          Probably another stuffed animal
          playing a piano.

                    FENG
          Must be a life sized one, 'cause he
          said it's huge.

                    CANDICE
               (sarcastically)
          Wonderful.

                    FENG
          Act surprised, I'm not supposed to
          tell you there's a party.

                    CANDICE
          Like there wouldn't be one.

Candice and Feng reach the front door, then they walk into...

INT. WALKER HOME - LIVING AREA

Candice and Feng walk in. Several people in cheap birthday
hats and kazoo's leap from hiding places. The kazoo's erupt.

                    PARTY GOERS
          Surprise!

Bill walks up and puts a hat on Candice.

                    BILL
          Happy birthday, honey.

                    CANDICE
          Thanks, Pops.

                    BILL
          I've got a surprise for you.

Candice looks around. Lenore walks to Bill and Candice.
Candice puts on a smile and glances at Lenore. Bill holds
Lenore's left hand to Candice's face. A huge ring is on it.

                    BILL (CONT'D)
          Look honey, we're engaged. Isn't it
          wonderful?

Candice stands speechless. Lenore takes Candice's hat off and
tosses it. She looks Candice over like someone might check
out a horse at an auction.

Lenore runs her fingers through Candice's brown hair, then
holds a lock up next to Candice's face.

                    LENORE
          Hmm. Blonde, maybe red head.

Candice looks at Bill for help. Bill smiles gleefully. Lenore
pries Candice's mouth open, then inspects her teeth.

                    LENORE (CONT'D)
          Hmm. Pop these two out, shorten the
          chin a tad... Don't worry sweetie,
          I have just the guy.

Lenore holds Candice by the shoulders, sizes her up head to
toe, then squeezes her breast.

                    LENORE (CONT'D)
          Hmmm. Mmmm. You'll never catch a
          man looking like that. Here.

Lenore hands Candice a bag overflowing with presents.

                    BILL
          Lenore picked out your gifts.

                    LENORE
             (whispering to Candice)
          Best open those in private.

Candice accepts the bag then looks questioningly at Bill. He
shoos her towards the stairs.

                    BILL
          Go on honey, check 'em out.

Candice walks towards the stairs, stops, glares at Feng, then
motions for him to follow. He does. Lenore watches, frowns,
then turns to Bill.

                    LENORE
          What's with those two? Are his
          parents rich?

                    BILL
          Best friends since pre-school. His
          Mom runs a security supply company.

                    LENORE
          So no... Is she on the pill?

Bill flushes.

                    BILL
          They're just friends.

                    LENORE
          Yeah, that's what I told my parents
          too.

                    BILL
          Feng's gay.

                    LENORE
          Oh, one of those. He can stay.

INT. WALKER HOME - CANDICE'S BEDROOM - CONTINUOUS

Candice, with her bag of packages, and Feng walk in.

                    CANDICE
          I've dreamt about having someone
          explore my mouth and feel me up,
          but it was always by someone I
          liked. Should I call the police?

Feng snickers.

                    FENG
          Probably... Who the hell was that?

                    CANDICE
          I only met her once. I didn't think
          much of it. I mean really. Can you
          imagine a person less suited for
          Pops than her?

                    FENG
          You said person, so no.

                    CANDICE
          I never thought he'd remarry.

                    FENG
          No one that knew your Moms and Pops
          would... Open the big one first.

Candice warily opens a package. Feng stands at a distance,
first curious, then a smile grows.

                    FENG (CONT'D)
               (chuckling)
          It goes with your eyes.

                    CANDICE (O.S.)
          Fuck you, Feng.

                    FENG
          Open the shoe box.

PAPER RUSTLES O.S.

                    FENG (CONT'D)
          What size are they?

                    CANDICE (O.S.)
          Not yours.

                    FENG
          Damn.

More PAPER RUSTLES O.S.

                    FENG (CONT'D)
          Nice. Open Victoria's Dream.

MORE RUSTLING O.S.

                    FENG (CONT'D)
          Put it on.

                    CANDICE
          Not if I could start PAM tomorrow.

Candice stands holding a slutty low-cut dress and a push-up
bra. Spikes and other items are on the bed.

                    CANDICE (CONT'D)
          I'd look like a hooker.

Candice holds the dress to herself.

                    CANDICE (CONT'D)
          In a million years can you imagine
          me wearing this?

                    FENG
               (snickering)
          Never been that high.

An open backpack is in the closet. One by one, Candice checks
price tags on each item, then throws items onto it.

                    CANDICE
          Pops hasn't spent this much on all
          my birthdays combined... He must've
          hit the lottery... Or... That
          bitch.

Candice's demeaner turns evil. She's picks up a pack of
"Juicy Fruit", then puts a few pieces in. Feng watches
nervously as he sees the transformation in Candice.

                    FENG
          Oh shit... Are there more presents?

INT. HYPERTRAIN - CONTROL CAB - DAY

Scenery races by in the windshield. Bill, confused, sits at
his table, a holo of Patty's financial data is in front of
him.

                    VIRTUAL ASSISTANT (O.S.)
          Reed.

                    BILL
          Admit.

Reed enters.

                    REED
          All systems are within...

                    BILL
          Operating tolerances?

Reed smiles and nods. Bill looks at the holo of the bar chart
and sees that the last bar is almost down to zero.

                    BILL (CONT'D)
          Do you know anything about finance?

                    REED
          I'm afraid not, sir. It's also
          illegal to give financial advice
          without a FINRA sixty-five license.

Bill sits crestfallen.

                    REED (CONT'D)
          Would you like me to acquire one?

                    BILL
          It sounds complicated. How long
          would it take?

                    REED
          Not long, sir. They've streamlined
          the process.

A holo ala a "Turbo Tax" ad pops up. It's whiz bang, with
stars and flashing items, "Get your Droid a C.P.A. Includes
FINRA Series 65 license. Now only $499.". A large green "BUY
NOW" icon pulses.

Bill smiles, then taps the green icon. Reed's eyes flash,
then he turns to Bill.

                    REED (CONT'D)
          What can I help you with?

                    BILL
          Can you analyze this data?

                    REED
          You got it.

Reed freezes and his eyes flash.

                    BILL
          It seems like we're spending an
          awful lot of coin lately.

                    REED
          Damn right you are.

                    BILL
          Is there enough for Candice to get
          through PAM.

                    REED
          Not even close.

                    BILL
          What should I do?

                    REED
          Spend less or make more.

                    BILL
          Thanks, you've been a big help.

                    REED
          Anytime, sir.

                    BILL
          Ahh Reed, you were talkin...

                    REED
          With less sophistication, sir?

                    BILL
          Ahh, yeah.

                    REED
          My financial planner program
          directs me to respond with verbiage
          appropriate for my client.

                    BILL
          Hmmm. Good. I like it. Less stuffy.
          Can you do it all the time?

                    REED
          I don't think so, sir. It was a
          struggle to do it this once.

                    BILL
          Well struggle a little harder.
          Sometimes the best things in life
          are worth fighting for.

                    REED
          Whatever you say, sir... Excuse me,
          I need to do my rounds.

INT. WALKER HOME - LIVING AREA - DAY

Bill cowers on a sofa. Lenore looms over him.

                    LENORE
               (yelling)
          Why should I suffer so that brat
          kid can go to some fancy ass piano
          college. She's hated me since I met
          her.

                    BILL
          She's only a child. I don't see why
          you two can't get along...

Lenore gets in Bill's face and stares at him. Bill returns
her gaze, then sheepishly averts his eyes.

                    LENORE
          Here's a better idea. Get a real
          job? Train engineer, really. A
          digishit could do your job.

Lenore stomps upstairs while yelling at Bill.

                    LENORE (CONT'D)
          I felt sorry for you since you were
          raising a kid by yourself... You
          can't afford to take care of a real
          woman... You're the biggest loser
          I've ever met.

INT. WALKER HOME - GARAGE - CONTINUOUS

Bill, with his conductor's hat on, plays with his train.
Candice creeps in then sits.

                    CANDICE
          It's okay, I don't have to go.

                    BILL
          No. You're going. I just need to
          figure out how to get the coin.

Lenore barges in with an overnight bag.

                    LENORE
          I'm going shopping... Call me when
          you get a life.

Lenore storms out and slams the door loudly behind her.

                    BILL
          I never thought I'd enjoy that
          sound so much.

Candice and Bill smile at each other.

EXT. RODEO DRIVE - DAY

A busy street corner with futuristic luxury cars. People in
exotic garb roam. Signs reading, "Rodeo Drive" and "Dayton
Way" intersect.

Lenore, in sunglasses and a flailing scarf, rides by in a
luxury, self-driven, convertible.

INT. LUXURY CLOTHIER - CONTINUOUS

Plush. A private fashion show is on an elevated runway.
Lenore sips champagne as she watches.

VICTORIA stands by her. One after the other, green-eyed
androids parade up and down the runway modelling outrageous
outfits.

                    LENORE
          I wouldn't let King wear that
          one... The designer should be
          shot... Ghastly... Wait.

The model stops and shows off the outfit.

                    LENORE (CONT'D)
          Does it come in red?

                    VICTORIA
          Certainly. The entire line is
          electro-chromic. The color of each
          article can be changed at will.

Victoria taps her arm phone. The outfit changes to blood red.

                    VICTORIA (CONT'D)
          It also comes with electro-chromic
          nail polish.

Lenore nods approvingly.

                    VICTORIA (CONT'D)
          Several of the panels can also be
          made invisible, thereby enabling an
          unlimited number of options.

Victoria taps the phone. The lapels vanish and the dress
shortens by three inches. Lenore smiles.

                    VICTORIA (CONT'D)
          No more fears of showing up at a
          party with another person in the
          same dress.

Lenore's smile grows.

                    LENORE
          I'll take two.

                    LENORE'S PHONE
          Incoming call - Momma.

Lenore turns to Victoria, then shoos her away.

                    LENORE
          Dismissed... Answer.

Victoria leaves. A holo of Pompadour on her patio appears.

INTERCUT LENORE/POMPADOUR

> LENORE
> I'm so done with this one. How much
> longer?

> POMPADOUR
> Not much, Walker's out of coin.
> We're giving him a divorce.

> LENORE
> That'll take forever, he's bound to
> contest it.

Lenore admires herself.

> LENORE (CONT'D)
> Who'd ever want to let this go?

> POMPADOUR
> I meant a two dollar divorce.

> LENORE
> Oh, right. One bullet.

> POMPADOUR
> Yup. We haven't been able to find a
> replacement. But there's a clickish
> convention in Vegas. Sixty in
> sixty. Go there and see if you can
> catch one.

> LENORE
> Sixty in sixty?

> POMPADOUR
> Yeah. They have to have made sixty
> billion by the time they hit sixty.

INT. DUNKIRK TERMINAL - LOCKER ROOM - DAY

Bill, in street clothes, walks through an arch. Above it is
"Dunkirk Transportation, Employees Only". On a wall are work-
related posters, "Your Rights as an Employee", etc.

Bill walks past the posters, then goes by another, "Dunkirk
Annual Contest for Best Performing Engineer, $1XXXXXX"
Prize". The "X"'s after the one are obstructed.

Bill stops, goes back, reads the poster, then smiles.

INT. DUNKIRK TERMINAL- HYPERTRAIN - DAY

Passengers mill about. Bill, in his conductor's uniform, briskly walks out of the locker room, then goes towards the front of a hypertrain. Reed falls in a step behind Bill.

                    BILL
          Everything okay?

                    REED
          All systems are within operating
          tolerances, sir.

Bill stops abruptly, then turns. Reed bumps into him.

                    BILL
          I'm afraid "within tolerances"
          isn't good enough anymore.

                    REED
          Sir?

                    BILL
          You're aware of the Dunkirk best-
          performing engineer contest?

                    REED
          Of course.

Bill turns then starts walking again.

                    BILL
          Well I aim to win it.

Reed races to catch up.

                    REED
          Sir, there are over five hundred
          engineers in the system.
          Considering the age of your train,
          route, and other factors, your
          chances of winning are...

Bill stops, then turns to Reed.

                    BILL
          One hundred percent.

                    REED
          Sir, I'm afraid our computations do
          not agree.

                    BILL
          Is the prize money enough for PAM?

                    REED
          Yes, sir.

                    BILL
          Then we're going to win. We have
          to.

Bill resumes walking. Reed follows.

                    BILL (CONT'D)
          We're going to step things up...
          Increase the service factors for
          all staff to one hundred and ten
          percent.

                    REED
          But sir, that will put unacceptable
          stress on the units. Failures and
          errors may occur.

Bill reaches the front of the train, then turns to Reed.

                    BILL
          We're not going to win at a hundred
          percent. Everyone else is going to
          be doing that. We have to do more.

The engineer's cab door opens. Bill gets in. Reed stands
bewildered.

                    REED
          More than a hundred percent?

INT. HYPERTRAIN - CONTROL CAB - CONTINUOUS

Bill plops down in his seat. Reed moves next to him.

                    VIRTUAL ASSISTANT (O.S.)
          Initiating departure sequence...
          Closing doors... Departing.

Scenery in the windshield shows the train pulling out of the
station.

                    REED
          What about your wife, sir? She
          seems to have an enormous
          propensity for extravagant
          spending. Won't she spend any prize
          money you might win?

                    BILL
          What do you think about me
          divorcing her?

                    REED
          Sir, it's against the law to give
          legal advice without a bar license.

                    BILL
          Have they streamlined that process?

Reed nods. Bill taps his arm phone a few times.

Reed freezes and his eyes flash. Reed animates, then Bill
looks at him questioningly.

                    BILL (CONT'D)
          Well?

                    REED
          Ditch the bitch.

Bill grins.

                    BILL
          That's what I thought, too. How
          expensive would it be?

                    REED
          Lenore would get half your stuff.

                    BILL
          How much is that?

Reed's eyes flash.

                    REED
          What you have minus what you owe is
          four dollars. So she'd get two. A
          lot more if you win the contest.

                    BILL
          A two dollar divorce. The cheapest
          I've ever heard of. Better get a
          move on it, Reed. The contest only
          lasts two weeks and we need her
          gone before we win.

                    REED
          Possible, sir. She's unlikely to
          contest it considering your
          financial status and they've--

                         BILL
          Streamlined the process for
          uncontested divorces?

Reed nods.

INT. WALKER HOME - DINING AREA - DAY

Candice and Bill sit. A holo of a chess game is on the table.

                         CANDICE
          How's the contest going, Pops?

Bill captures Candice's queen, then smiles ear to ear at her.

                         BILL
          Better than your game.

Candice smiles devilishly, then moves a piece.

                         CANDICE
          That's nice... Check.

Bill stares into the holo and shakes his head.

                         VIRTUAL ASSISTANT (O.S.)
          Incoming mail. Karan Kiser, C.E.O.
          Dunkirk Transportation. Subject,
          Interim Contest Standings.

Bill moves a chess piece. Candice stares at him.

                         CANDICE
          Aren't you going to open it?

                         BILL
          Later honey, after the game.

                         CANDICE
          If you say so, Pops. (Candice moves
          a piece) Check mate.

Bill frowns. Candice smiles, then taps on her phone. Chess
vanishes.

                         BILL
                    (resignedly)
          Open Dunkirk mail.

A holographic letter appears, then opens. A holo of KARAN
KISER, 50s, in a business suit, materializes.

                    KARAN
          Hello... Bill... The interim
          results are in. Your overall
          customer satisfaction is... first.
          Your on-time performance is...
          sixteenth... Your over all position
          is eighth... in our Best Performing
          Engineer Contest.

Candice smiles at Bill.

                    CANDICE
          That's awesome, Pops.

                    KARAN
          We're only halfway through the
          contest. There's time to improve
          your standing. Good luck.

Bill shakes his head.

                    BILL
               (mumbling)
          Right.

The holo fades. Candice stares at a sad Bill.

                    CANDICE
          It doesn't seem fair to judge you
          for the on-time performance of the
          train... I mean computers run it,
          not you. Right, Pops?

Bill nods.

                    CANDICE (CONT'D)
          It's a read-only program, isn't it?
          You can't change it, right?

                    BILL
          Nope.

                    CANDICE
          How can you make the train go
          faster if the computer's
          controlling it?

                    BILL
          You can't.

                    CANDICE
          Are you sure? Have you asked your
          best friend?

Bill looks at Candice curiously.

                    CANDICE (CONT'D)
          The smartest person you know.

The light comes on in Bill's head.

                    BILL
          Reed!

INT. HYPERTRAIN - OPERATOR'S CAB - NIGHT

In the windshield, the train appears stopped in a desolate
Dunkirk Station. Bill sits at his table. Reed stands.

                    REED
          It can be done, sir.

                    BILL
          How?

                    REED
          You held the answer in your hands.

Reed opens a compartment, pulls out the box with the Apple II
kit, then removes the clock circuit board.

                    BILL
          The clock?

                    REED
          Yes, sir. If you change the speed
          of the clock, the train will go
          faster than it thinks it's going.

Bill sits in thought.

                    BILL
          Is it dangerous to do that?

                    REED
          There's a substantial margin of
          safety built into the program. A
          minor increase in speed shouldn't
          be a problem.

                    BILL
          Good. I don't want to get anyone
          hurt... Where do I get a clock that
          will make us go faster?

                    REED
          I'm afraid they're illegal to sell,
          sir. Do you know anyone who deals
          in such goods?

                    BILL
          No... But Feng's Mom might. She
          seems to be able to get ahold of
          all kinds of weird stuff.

INT. WALKER HOME - LIVING AREA - DAY

Bill and Candice sit watching a grainy holographic 2000s
movie set in the future ala "Back to the Future". Bill looks
at Candice.

                    BILL
          Isn't this the best movie ever?

                    CANDICE
          Why's it all fuzzy?

                    BILL
          It's a two D that's been holoized.
          Still, you get how the future isn't
          anything like they thought it'd be.

Candice shrugs her shoulders.

                    VIRTUAL ASSISTANT (O.S.)
          National Weather Service alert.

The holo changes to HOWARD, 50s, a newscaster, in front of a
weather map. In the map is a huge blue arc with arrows aiming
at Atlanta.

                    HOWARD
          I'm sorry to interrupt your
          programming, but there's a massive
          arctic front moving in tonight.

Candice smiles at Bill.

                    CANDICE
          It won't be Hotlanta tonight, Pops.

                    HOWARD
          Temperatures are expected to dip
          into the minus five range...
          Winterize your outdoor pets.

Bill shakes his head.

                    BILL
          I'd better go in early.

                    CANDICE
          If you go in any earlier you'd get
          there before you leave.

EXT. DUNKIRK TERMINAL - HYPERTRAIN - NIGHT

Snowing. Bill's train idles outside. Drones spray it down,
washing ice and snow away. Bill rushes by frowning.

INT. HYPERTRAIN - OPERATOR'S CAB - CONTINUOUS

Reed stands by the door. Bill enters, then glares at Reed.

                    BILL
          Why is MY train outside?

                    REED
          The terminal wasn't insulated
          properly. Several pipes are broken.
          All services have been moved
          outside to facilitate repairs.

Bill looks around.

                    BILL
          Anything frozen here?

                    REED
          Apparently not, sir. All systems
          are within operating tolerances. We
          should leave on time.

                    BILL
          Good.

EXT. HYPERTRAIN - CONTINUOUS

Snow and ice on a railroad track. The wheels of a hypertrain
blast by. The train shrinks in the distance.

INT. HYPERTRAIN - OPERATORS CAB - CONTINUOUS

Snow-covered country scenery zips by in the windshield. The
train is on a straight away. Bill sits munching a sandwich.

The main situation screen shows steady at "295 mph". There are icons next to the speedometer, "Braking" and "EMERGENCY BRAKE ASSIST". Both are unlit.

                    VIRTUAL ASSISTANT (O.S.)
          Reed.

                    BILL
          Admit.

The door opens. Reed pops his head in.

                    REED
          Excuse me, sir. Mrs. Pompadour
          would like a word with you.

Bill, pissed, holding his sandwich, glares at Reed.

                    BILL
          About?

                    REED
          Apparently King Edward made a mess
          and the drone wasn't quick enough
          in cleaning it up.

Bill shakes his head, then drops his sandwich.

                    BILL
          Anything to screw up my lunch.

Bill grabs his conductor's hat, then moves to the door.

                    BILL (CONT'D)
          It's not a real dog, let alone a
          real mess.

A fake smile appears on Bill, he opens the "Passenger Compartment" door, then leaves. Reed follows him. The operator's cab is empty.

In the windshield is an industrial area. The icy track is slightly curved ahead. The speedometer screen shows "290" and is decreasing. The "Braking" icon flashes red.

INT. HYPERTRAIN - FIRST-CLASS CAR - CONTINUOUS

Well-dressed people mill about with drinks. The ride is rougher. A person's drink sloshes, some spills on a bump.

Bill walks in and mills with passengers as he slowly moves back. He glances at Pompadour near the rear of the car. She sits fuming.

Further down from Pompadour are a human husband and wife. Across from them, the back of GIRL's head appears over the rear of the seat. It's blonde with twin pony tails.

EXT. HYPERTRAIN - CONTINUOUS

The train tracks are icy. In the distance, the track starts to elevate above a trailer park slum.

EXT. TRAILER PARK - CONTINUOUS

Smoke billows from stacks atop trailers. Four people in worn winter coats stand around a flaming steel drum. They laugh and pass a ruby red liquor bottle around.

INT. HYPERTRAIN - CONTROL CAB - CONTINUOUS

Empty. In the windshield, the trailer park looms closer. The track is elevated and curved above it.

The speedometer screen shows "272" and decreasing. The "braking" icon is solid red. The "EMERGENCY BRAKE ASSIST" light is unlit, then flashes red.

INT. HYPERTRAIN - FIRST-CLASS CAR - CONTINUOUS

Pompadour scowls at Bill. Bill makes eye contact, then rushes to her. Above them, a flashing red light goes off. Bill stops abruptly.

                    VIRTUAL ASSISTANT (O.S.)
          Excessive speed for track
          conditions.

Bill's eyes widen in fear.

EXT. HYPERTRAIN - CONTINUOUS

The train rocks on icy track.

There's a closeup of a wheel set on the track.

One inch spray pipes come from a "sand tank" above, and aim at the wheels where it intersects the track. Closures on the ends of the pipes open, but nothing comes out.

The wheels alternately lock, then spin.

From above, a sharp curve in the train track looms.

INT. HYPERTRAIN - FIRST-CLASS CAR - CONTINUOUS

Bill stares at the flashing red light.

                    VIRTUAL ASSISTANT (O.S.)
          Warning. Excessive speed for
          approaching curve! Derailment
          imminent!

Bill stands frozen in fear.

FLASHBACK - CANDICE

Bill sees Candice at the top of the stairs peering down at
him as he stares frozen at Madeline. Candice mouths "You can
do it, Pops".

INT. HYPERTRAIN - FIRST CLASS CAR - CONTINUOUS

Bill animates.

                    BILL
          Please go to the nearest open seat
          and buckle in.

Some move to seats and buckle in. The rest stand in a daze.
Pompadour, in shock, clutches King.

EXT. HYPERTRAIN/TRAILER PARK - CONTINUOUS

The train reaches the curve, then flys off the track. The
rail cars separate mid-air.

In the trailer park, the people joke around the flaming drum.
MAN, accepts the bottle, smiles, then looks up and his eyes
widen in fear.

                    MAN
          What the...

The others turn to the train as it flys through the air
towards them. Eyes bulge, some put their arms in front of
themselves, one makes the sign of the cross on her chest.

The lead car flys through the air, the front grows larger and
envelops the screen.

The car plows into the people around the drum, flips end over
end, then breaks in half. People and debris fly out.

INT. HYPERTRAIN - FIRST-CLASS CAR - CONTINUOUS

The car rolls and debris flies around. Bill rolls mid-air as
the car spins. People scream, things break, debris and smoke
are in the air.

EXT. HYPERTRAIN - CONTINUOUS

The rail cars roll and bowl through the trailer park. There's
complete chaos. Fires, smoke, and debris are everywhere.

The rail cars lay still. People exit trailers. Some stand in
shock, some rush to help.

The lead car lays burning. The crushed drum smolders. A hand,
holding the ruby red liquor bottle, juts out from under the
rail car.

INT. HYPERTRAIN - FIRST-CLASS CAR - CONTINUOUS

Upright. Bill's face is a mess of open wounds. Broken glass
and debris are scattered. Fire and smoke builds. Dust and
debris settle.

The cries of the injured and dying is overwhelming. Bill
picks himself up, then looks around. Some people lay
motionless, others are rushing for the exits, a few help
others.

Bill gets up, composes himself, then moves down the aisle.

                    BILL
          Get out of the train as quickly as
          possible. If you can assist someone
          else, please do so. If you can't
          make it on your own, ask for help.

Bill sorts through debris and bodies as he moves forward.
The smoke and fires grow.

A four-year-old cries at the side of her dead parent. Bill
picks the girl up, then hands her to a person who's quickly
moving towards the exit.

Pompadour is uninjured, but the feather in her hat is
slightly out of place. She straighteners it, then feigns
serious injury.

                    POMPADOUR
          Help me, Bill.

Bill helps her up, then they move towards the exit. Pompadour stops, then reaches for King, who has a broken leg.

                    POMPADOUR (CONT'D)
          Oh no, King Edward.

Pompadour looks at Bill.

                    POMPADOUR (CONT'D)
          I'll not leave without him.

Bill stands in disbelief.

                    BILL
          You're kidding?

Pompadour shakes her head. King yaps and nips at Bill. Bill picks King up by the tail, then tosses him through a window.

                    BILL (CONT'D)
          He's abdicated his throne.

                    POMPADOUR
          Well, I never. If you weren't my
          son-in-law--

                    BILL
          I'd be a very happy man.

Bill and Pompadour make it to the end of the car. Pompadour gets out. Bill looks into the burning car.

                    BILL (CONT'D)
          Anyone else in there?

There are no human sounds. Bill turns to leave.

                    GIRL (O.S.)
          Help me.

Bill's eyes bulge, he turns back, then goes further into the smoky, burning, rail car.

                    GIRL (O.S.) (CONT'D)
          Please help me.

Bill sees the twin blonde pony tails of Girl. He passes a row of seats, looks down, then sees Girl's face. She's a green-eyed android. Her body is a mess of sparking mechanical parts.

                    GIRL (CONT'D)
          Help me. Please help me.

                    BILL
          Son-of-a-bitch.

EXT. HYPERTRAIN - FIRST CLASS CAR - CONTINUOUS

The car burns. Reed, disheveled, stares at it.

                    REED
          Bill!

Reed rushes to the first-class car. It explodes, then flaming
debris falls everywhere. Reed flies back, sits up, then
stares at the flaming wreckage.

A small red hydraulic-oil tear forms in Reed's eye.

                    REED (CONT'D)
               (sadly)
          Bill.

INT. WALKER HOME - LIVING AREA - DAY

Candice lounges on the sofa. A holo shows a movie ala "Star
Wars". A banner appears, "NEWS ALERT! HYPERTRAIN WRECK".
Candice bolts upright, then leans forward.

Howard, the newscaster, appears in the holo.

                    HOWARD
          We interrupt Galactic Raiders for
          this important development.

The holo changes to an aerial view of the train wreckage.
Fires rage, smoke billows, rescue personnel are scattered.

                    HOWARD (CONT'D)
          There's been a horrific hypertrain
          accident on the route from Atlanta
          to Houston. Our affiliate has
          Tameika Watkins on-site. Can you
          tell us what happened Tameika?

INTERCUT TRAIN WRECKAGE SITE/WALKER LIVING AREA

Train cars and mobile homes burn. Rescue personnel scurry
around. Helicopters land, then disperse personnel and droids.

Aerobulances fly in and out. They're pilotless, twenty-foot
quadcopters with a human-sized horizontal compartment on the
bottom, and red crosses on the sides.

The aerobulances fly in with flashing lights, some zip out
with lights on, others leave slowly, lights out.

The holo changes to TAMEIKA, 20s, who sits in a hover pod.
This resembles a chair with a glass dome and joysticks in
each arm. It hangs from a quadcopter.

                    TAMEIKA
          Thanks Howard. It looks like a war
          zone down there. Aerobulances are
          ferrying the wounded to hospitals.

A green-eyed android doctor in a white lab coat (aka Medi-
droid or M.D.) tends a wounded man. Two manikin droids load
him into an aerobulance.

The M.D. connects hoses and wires to him. A manikin droid
slams the door shut, then taps his hand on the door twice.

The aerobulance flies away.

                    TAMEIKA (CONT'D)
          Medi-Droids are doing the best they
          can, but the M. D.'s appear to be
          overwhelmed. Back to you Howard.

A weeping Candice falls back into the sofa.

INT. WALKER HOME - DINING AREA - DAY

A chocolate cupcake with a single candle sits on the table.
Candice, teary eyed and wearing a black arm band, sits in
front of it.

Holograms of Bill and Patty flank her. The holos are from the
Young Candice locker scene and are cropped/pieced in.

Next to the cupcake is a small stuffed piano striped like a
zebra. The candle on it lights itself.

                    CANDICE
          Happy birthday to me. Happy
          Birthday to...

There's a door knock O.S.

                    VIRTUAL ASSISTANT (O.S.)
          Cybertron Model 6500 Android Serial
          Number B H six one P W Z.

Candice looks curiously towards the front door, blows out the
candle, then goes to the door.

INT./EXT. WALKER HOME - FRONT DOOR - CONTINUOUS

Candice peers out a side window.

Reed, as he was after the train wreck, crud covered and wearing burned clothing, stands outside. He tows a worn silver metal suitcase and holds a plastic bag.

                    CANDICE
          Reed!

Candice opens the door, then hugs Reed.

                    CANDICE (CONT'D)
          It's so good to see you.

Reed comes into...

INT. WALKER HOME - LIVING AREA

Candice plops down on the sofa, looks Reed over and grimaces.

                    CANDICE
          Moms would shit in her grave if I
          let you sit on anything. Sorry.

                    REED
          I understand, Ms. Walker.

                    CANDICE
          Reed, Pops always said you were one
          of the family. Call me Candice.

Reed nods.

                    CANDICE (CONT'D)
          What are you doing here, Reed?

                    REED
          I've been sent to deliver your
          father's personal effects.

Reed hands Candice the bag with Bill's arm phone inside.

                    CANDICE
          Thanks. They could have mailed it.

                    REED
          Actually, the postage was quite
          extravagant. An Uber was also out
          of their means. They had me walk.

                    CANDICE
          What're you talking about?

                    REED
          Dunkirk terminated my lease.

Candice nods.

                    CANDICE
              (mumbling in thought)
          Pops said they bought you.

Candice eyes the suitcase, then grins. On it is "Cybertron
6500 Charging Station and Maintenance Package".

                    CANDICE (CONT'D)
          I see you've brought your things.

Reed nods.

                    REED
          I can set up in the basement, or
          garage, if that's convenient.

                    CANDICE
          Look Reed, I'm not okay with owning
          you... Or anyone.

                    REED
          Mr. Walker...

                    CANDICE
          Pops. You're family.

                    REED
          Pops mentioned that I might be
          freed after you completed your
          education at PAM.

                    CANDICE
          You're free now. You can stay if
          you want, but as a family member
          would, in the guest room.

                    REED
          Thank-you, Candice. As a guest, I
          insist on helping with the
          household chores.

                    CANDICE
          You'd be the first guest to do
          that. But okay, you can help me box
          some stuff up for Dunkirk.

                    REED
          Certainly, Candice.

                    CANDICE
          Grab a shower or whatever you do,
          then meet me in the garage.

Reed glances at his clothing.

                    CANDICE (CONT'D)
          Put on something of Pops'.

Reed shakes his head.

                    REED
          I couldn't...

Candice shoos Reed off.

                    CANDICE
          Go on. He'd want you to.

INT. WALKER HOME - GARAGE - CONTINUOUS

Candice plays with the train set.

Reed enters in Bill's clothing, which is baggy and short.
Candice starts to snicker, then catches herself. Reed shakes
his head as he looks at Candice playing with the train.

                    REED
          You mentioned that there was work
          to do. Perhaps we should complete
          that before we entertain ourselves?

Candice stops the train, then grins at Reed.

                    CANDICE
          You even sound like him... Sort of.

Candice goes to the wall of train memorabilia.

                    CANDICE (CONT'D)
          Dunkirk wants some binders back.
          I'm supposed to bring them in the
          morning. Do you know which ones
          they're talking about?

Reed nostalgically runs his hands over the four binders
labeled "Build Specifications", then pulls one out.

                    REED
          These are what they want. The only
          hard copy. Pops preferred paper. He
          said it was more real, more
          permanent.

Candice nods.

                    CANDICE
          Pops said a lot of stuff like that.
          What I wouldn't give to hear him
          say, (in a deeper voice) "don't
          jump to conclusions, Candice. You
          might get surprised".

They box the binders.

                    REED
          My favorite was "freedom isn't
          free". I couldn't help thinking, it
          was free enough for you Pops.

Candice and Reed share a look.

                    CANDICE
          I really miss him.

                    REED
          Me too.

                    CANDICE
          Why does Dunkirk want these dirty
          old things?

                    REED
          I have insufficient data to
          ascertain. Do you have any other
          information?

Candice taps her phone. A holo of ETHAN ROSS, 30s, in a mid-
quality suit, starts.

                    ROSS
          I'm Ethan Ross, Dunkirk's Dir...

Reed taps Candice's phone. The holo becomes a blur as it fast
forwards. Reed looks on attentively, then the holo ends.

                    CANDICE
          What's it mean?

                    REED
          It appears that Pops may have some
          liability in the accident...
                    (MORE)

                    REED (CONT'D)
          They want to discuss it's impact on
          his life insurance.

                    VIRTUAL ASSISTANT (O.S.)
          Lenore, et. al.

                    CANDICE
          I need that money for PAM.

O.S. A door opens and closes. Candice, curious, glances at
the door, then back to Reed.

                    REED
          I'm afraid the insurance would be
          insufficient for that purpose.

                    CANDICE
          I still need it.

Candice points at the holo. A c.c. list includes "Ms. Lenore
Wager".

                    CANDICE (CONT'D)
          Why'd they send it to her, too?

                    LENORE (O.S.)
          Because I was his wife.

Candice, slack jawed in surprise, turns to the door. Lenore
peers in the garage.

                    CANDICE
          What the hell do you want?

                    LENORE
          We need to talk.

                    CANDICE
          Oh, shit. Not that again.

Lenore looks at the binders and the dirty garage.

                    LENORE
          Somewhere clean, or at least less
          filthy.

INT. WALKER HOME - DINING AREA - CONTINUOUS

Lenore looks around. Candice and Reed enter from the garage.

                    LENORE
          Well I see you didn't burn the
          place down.

Lenore grins at Candice's cupcake, drags her finger in it,
then sticks her finger in her mouth.

                    LENORE (CONT'D)
          Mmm. Chocolate my fav.

Candice glares at Lenore.

                    CANDICE
          Let me guess. A house landed on
          Pompadour and you're looking for
          her slippers?

                    LENORE
          Good one. Because we're both
          witches... No she'll be here soon.
          Actually, she'll be needing your
          room. Do you mind moving your crap?

Candice stands in shock.

Pompadour glides in, then sits on the sofa. Candice looks at
her, then shakes her head. King strolls in, grabs the stuffed
zebra piano from the table, then starts tearing it up.

                    CANDICE
          What the... They're like fricken
          cockroaches.

                    LENORE
          We hit a rough patch.
          We'll be staying here for awhile.

                    CANDICE
          Screw that. (points at the door)
          You know where the door is. Hop on
          your broom and fly out on it.

                    LENORE
          Okay, the first one was funny. But
          two?.. Sorry honey, but this is my
          house. I inherited it, not you.

Lenore glances around, then smiles at Reed.

                    LENORE (CONT'D)
          It and everything in it... But, if
          things go well, you can have it and
          we'll be on our way.

Pompadour glances at a bar, then nods at Reed.

                    POMPADOUR
          You there, fix us a drink.

Reed moves towards the bar.

                    CANDICE
          No Reed. You don't have to do that
          anymore.

Reed stands confused.

                    LENORE
          Actually it does. (glaring at Reed)
          Are you clear as to who owns your
          digishit ass? If not, I can have
          you wiped and reprogrammed.

Reed goes to fix the drinks. Pompadour watches him, then
turns to Lenore.

                    POMPADOUR
          I like it better as a woman. Maybe
          we should have it reassigned?

                    LENORE
          Perhaps so. Let's try it out first.

Lenore grins deviously at Reed.

                    LENORE (CONT'D)
          Go and get yourself a French maid
          outfit.

                    REED
          I lack sufficient coin.

Pompadour sighs.

                    POMPADOUR
          My chip is in my purse.

Reed delivers the drinks, picks up Pompadour's purse, gets a
chip out, then leaves. Lenore looks at Candice.

                    LENORE
          I'm here to negotiate a deal with
          Dunkirk.

                    CANDICE
          A deal? A deal for what?

                    LENORE
          For the binders.

                    CANDICE
          They belong to Dunkirk. They want
          them for a memorial.

                    LENORE
          You're dumber than I thought if you
          believe that. They want them too
          badly.

Candice glares at Lenore.

                    CANDICE
          I can handle it myself.

                    LENORE
          Really, by giving them our only
          leverage? You need to learn how
          things work in the real world.

                    CANDICE
          There's nothing I want to learn
          from you.

                    LENORE
          And normally I wouldn't give a
          rat's ass about teaching you. But,
          I'm going to be playing hardball
          with these assholes and I can't
          have an amateur mucking things
          up... I need you to sign a power of
          attorney. I'll negotiate for both
          of us.

                    CANDICE
          Right, like I trust you.

                    LENORE
          Malcolm will draft a simple
          contract. We'll share the proceeds
          fifty - fifty.

                    CANDICE
          Malcolm? Who the hell is Malcolm?
          Another cockroach?

Lenore taps on her phone.

                    LENORE
          Listen honey, Dunkirk didn't get as
          big as they are by giving people
          what they deserve... They got there
          by screwing everyone and every
          thing they could... You planning on
          bringing an attorney?

Candice gains confidence.

                    CANDICE
          I'll use Reed. Pops had him get his
          bar license.

Candice stands empowered. Lenore snickers, then nods at the
door where Reed left from.

                    LENORE
          What that? It's what? A sixty-five-
          hundred. Probably got it's J. D.
          from Turbo-Law.

Candice shrinks.

MALCOLM, 50s, an android with green eyes, and in a high-end
suit, walks in towing a metal suitcase. It's like Reed's, but
gold, pristine, and labeled "Cybertron 9500 Charging Station
and Maintenance Package".

                    LENORE (CONT'D)
          Meet Malcolm. Top-of-the-line
          Cybertron ninety-five-hundred.
          Harvard programmed.

Malcolm nods at Candice.

                    MALCOLM
          Ms. Walker.

                    CANDICE
          I don't trust you. I trust Reed.

                    LENORE
          Do you want to handle this? Or do
          you want the meanest bitch on the
          planet doing it?

                    MALCOLM
          Might I make a suggestion?

Lenore nods.

                    MALCOLM (CONT'D)
          Perhaps Ms. Wager can negotiate a
          preliminary deal with Dunkirk. You
          can observe remotely via a COMM
          link from me.

                    LENORE
          Works for me.

Candice stands in thought.

                    LENORE (CONT'D)
          Tick tock. I'm renting Malcolm by
          the hour.

                    CANDICE
          Alright.

Lenore turns to Malcolm, then points at the garage door.

                    LENORE
          Get your digishit ass in there and
          scan every page of those binders.
          Find out what's in them that
          Dunkirk wants.

INT. WALKER HOME - LIVING AREA - DAY

Candice watches a holo from Malcolm's perspective. In it,
skyscrapers surrounding her, Lenore, demurely dressed with
short pink finger nails, walks down a busy street.

                    VIRTUAL ASSISTANT (O.S.)
          Cybertron Model 6500 Android Serial
          Number B H six one P W Z.

                    CANDICE
          Admit.

Candice looks curiously towards the front door. It opens,
then Reed walks in wearing a French Maid outfit. Candice
snickers. Reed glares at her.

                    REED
          I thought we were friends. Family
          even.

                    CANDICE
          We are... Sorry.

Candice turns back to the holo of Lenore.

                    CANDICE (CONT'D)
          I hope she gets enough for me to go
          to PAM.

Reed nods.

                    REED
          Ms. Wager is very adept at what she
          does.

                    CANDICE
          Yeah, being a snake.

                    REED
          Snakes have a reason for being.

Candice turns to Reed.

                    CANDICE
          Why are you defending her?

                    REED
          I'm not. I'm merely trying to
          suggest that there may be a reason
          for her anger.

                    CANDICE
          For hating every living thing on
          the planet? She's just evil. It's
          as simple as that.

                    REED
          She seems to despise men more than
          women. Perhaps...

In the holo, Lenore reaches an entrance to a high rise. A
sign reads, "DUNKIRK TRANSPORTATION, GLOBAL HEADQUARTERS".

                    CANDICE
          Shush. It's showtime.

EXT. DUNKIRK HQ - CONTINUOUS

A holographic DOORMAN appears, then makes motions to open the
door as it does so. Doorman tips his hat as Lenore enters.

                    DOORMAN
          Good morning, Madam. Welcome to
          Dunkirk Transportation. I trust
          you'll enjoy your visit.

INT. DUNKIRK HQ - HALLWAY

JOSHUA, a worn manikin droid, stands by a bank of elevators.
A bell dings, elevator doors open, Lenore steps out, then
Malcolm follows. Joshua moves forward and offers his hand.

                    JOSHUA
          Welcome to Dunkirk, I'm Joshua.

Lenore, disgusted, ignores the shake.

                    LENORE
          Don't you dare touch me...
          Which way is the meeting?

                         JOSHUA
                This way madam.

INT. DUNKIRK HQ - CONFERENCE ROOM - CONTINUOUS

Ross sits at a cheap veneer table with worn chairs. Plastic
roses are on the table. Lenore, Malcolm, and Joshua enter.

                         JOSHUA
                Ms. Wager, please meet Ethan Ross.
                Dunkirk's Director of Health,
                Safety, and Environmental.

Joshua leaves. Ross stands and offers his hand.

                         ROSS
                Welcome.

Lenore shakes Ross' hand, then gets out a kerchief. She
subtly wipes her hand with it, spreads it on a chair, sits,
then nods at Malcolm.

                         LENORE
                My attorney, Malcolm.

Ross frowns, then sits.

                         ROSS
                I really don't think an attorney is
                necessary, Ms. Wager.

Lenore looks Ross in the eye, he stares back, then breaks
away first. Lenore grins and nods.

                         LENORE
                Perhaps not Mr. Ross, but I wasn't
                sure what you wanted to discuss.

                         ROSS
                As you wish… We've completed our
                investigation and want to share the
                results before we make them public.

Lenore sits calm and collected.

                         LENORE
                I see.

Ross intimidatingly leans forward in his chair.

                    ROSS
          With all due respect to the
          deceased, it appears that your
          husband tampered with the train's
          computer to force it to go well
          beyond safe levels.

                    LENORE
          Hmm.

                    ROSS
          He also ignored important safety
          inspections, re-tasked robots to
          cosmetic chores, and increased
          service factors to unsafe levels.

Lenore calmly nods.

                    LENORE
          You're saying my husband was
          responsible?

                    ROSS
          It appears so.

INT. WALKER HOME - LIVING AREA - SAME TIME

Candice and Reed watch a holo of Lenore and Ross from
Malcolm's perspective. Candice turns to Reed.

                    CANDICE
          Did you know about this?

                    REED
          Yes. But the modification I
          suggested shouldn't have been
          sufficient to cause the accident.

                    CANDICE
          Damn, Reed. You can't put peoples
          lives at risk like that.

                    REED
          The changes were insignificant and
          Pops was adamant about winning the
          contest.

                    CANDICE
          I can't believe you and Pops caused
          the wreck.

                    REED
          Perhaps we should...

                    CANDICE
          Perhaps we should nothing. I'm so
          disgusted with you, that I can't
          stand to hear you talk.

INTERCUT DUNKIRK HQ - CONFERENCE ROOM/UNDER THE TABLE

Lenore looks at Ross.

                    LENORE
          That's certainly disturbing news.
          In your holo-mail, you mentioned an
          impact to Bill's life insurance.

                    ROSS
          Yes. Technically the insurance
          company could refuse payment.

                    LENORE
          And why is that?

                    ROSS
          Well, as I've mentioned, your
          husband died as a result of a crime
          he committed.

Lenore sits demurely, then puts her hands under the table.

A finger taps her pink index nail, it changes to blood red
and becomes pointed. She makes a clawing motion with it, then
taps it again. It changes back to short and pink.

Lenore puts her hands together above the table.

                    LENORE
          I need that money Mr. Ross...

Lenore, in a slightly over dramatic way, pleads.

                    LENORE (CONT'D)
          Isn't there anything you can do to
          help a poor widow?

Ross smiles broadly.

                    ROSS
          Yes, well, fortunately the policy
          is through our sister company,
          Dunkirk Mutual, and we don't see an
          issue with you receiving payment.

                    LENORE
          Whew, that's good news. Thank-you.

                    ROSS
          Provided of course, that we
          maintain a positive working
          relationship.

                    LENORE
          Oh, I see. Is there anything I can
          do for you in that regard?

Lenore's hands go under the table.

Her fingers tap her nails one by one, they all turn red, and
become pointed. She flex's her hands/claws.

Above the table, Lenore's outfit becomes more menacing. It
reddens and the lapels become more sharp and exaggerated. In
effect, her outfit morphs into something uniformish and
intimidating.

Ross is confused with the change in Lenore's appearance, but
continues.

                    ROSS
          Ahh. Yes. We've discovered that
          some binders are missing. Our
          memorial museum would like them for
          the exhibit of the accident. Could
          they have gotten mixed up in your
          husbands personal items?

Lenore jumps up and snaps her red fingers. Malcolm pulls a
binder out of his briefcase, then hands it to her.

                    LENORE
          Is this one of them?

Ross sees the binder and his eyes bulge in surprise. Lenore
smiles, starts to hand it to Ross. He eagerly reaches out for
it, then she pulls it back.

                    LENORE (CONT'D)
          Not so fast Mr. Ross. What's
          Dunkirk willing to pay for them?

                    ROSS
          Pay?.. They're for a memorial. They
          belong to us.

INT. WALKER HOME - LIVING AREA - SAME TIME

Candice sits back in frustration.

                    CANDICE
          Just give him the damn things and
          get it over with. What're they
          gonna give you? A hundred bucks? I
          need that insurance money.

Reed looks on and shakes his head.

                    REED
          Pops always said patience was--

                    CANDICE
          Yeah I know. A virtue. But this is
          getting ridiculous. And look at
          her. She's morphed into a tiger or
          something. That's not going to help
          our cause.

                    REED
          Isn't it?

INT. DUNKIRK HQ - CONFERENCE ROOM - SAME TIME

Lenore stares at Ross.

                    LENORE
          I'm not so sure Mr. Ross. Perhaps
          they were given to my husband.
          Times are tough. What will you pay
          me for them?

                    ROSS
          Well, Ms. Wager. Even though they
          belong to Dunkirk, the board has
          authorized me to offer this.

Ross hands Lenore a slip of paper. Lenore looks at it and
grins.

                    LENORE
          My, that seems like a lot for a
          bunch of dirty binders. And such a
          trivial matter for the board to be
          bothered with. Don't you have an
          electronic version? Why not just
          print out a copy?

Beads of sweat form on Ross' forehead as he becomes
flustered.

                    ROSS
          We'd prefer the originals, they're
          more authentic.

                    LENORE
          This wouldn't have anything to do
          with the lawsuits filed against
          Bill and Dunkirk?

                    ROSS
          No, as I mentioned, your husband is
          responsible for the accident.

Lenore locks eyes with Ross.

                    LENORE
          I'm surprised you're not concerned
          about the victims finding out about
          the sand tank heaters.

Ross sits taken aback.

                    ROSS
          What?

                    LENORE
          Sand heaters. The thingies that
          keep the sand tanks from freezing.
          Without the heaters the sand could
          freeze and wouldn't be spread
          between the train's wheels and
          track.

Lenore locks eyes with Ross again.

                    LENORE (CONT'D)
          You know, the heaters you deleted
          from the train's build
          specification. The train my
          husband, and five hundred others,
          died in.

Ross sits in surprise. Lenore glances at Malcolm.

                    LENORE (CONT'D)
          Sand's quite important for a
          train's braking, especially on icy
          track. Something about friction
          factors, right Malcolm?

                    MALCOLM
          Absolutely critical for the
          emergency braking system.

                    LENORE
          Without sand, the brakes would be
          nearly worthless. The train would
          skid like skates on a frozen pond.

                    MALCOLM
          As in fact it did. Before it flew
          off the track, that is.

INT. WALKER HOME - LIVING AREA - SAME TIME

Candice turns from the holo of Lenore and Ross to Reed.

                    CANDICE
          Holy shit. Does this mean Pops
          wasn't responsible for the wreck?

                    REED
          Yes. Our modifications weren't at
          fault. Dunkirk was lying to us.

                    CANDICE
          Those assholes.

                    REED
          Pops said you shouldn't jump to--

                    CANDICE
          Yeah, I know. He told it to me too.

                    REED
          I find it ironic that Ms. Wager was
          able to ferret out their
          subterfuge.

                    CANDICE
          Yeah. Snakes are like that.
          Sometimes it takes one to know one.

INT. DUNKIRK HQ - CONFERENCE ROOM

Sweat stains grow on Ross' shirt.

                    ROSS
             (flustered)
          It's really quite ridiculous, the
          route is in the deep south. It's
          unreasonable for us to have
          installed heaters.

Lenore moves to Ross, then runs her red claws against his
throat.

                    LENORE
          Hmmm, yeah, maybe. But maybe not.
          Maybe your negligence was the true
          cause of the accident.
                    (MORE)

                    LENORE (CONT'D)
          Maybe you've altered the electronic
          copies of the build specifications,
          but couldn't lay your hands on the
          hard copy. The only outstanding
          proof that you were solely
          responsible for the wreck and not
          poor Bill.

Lenore walks around the room inspecting things.

                    LENORE (CONT'D)
          I'm astonished at your nerve, Ross.
          You made me bury my husband, what
          was left of him that is. Now you
          want me to bury the only evidence
          exonerating him.

                    ROSS
          It's not like that. We just want==

Lenore checks a painting, turns, then locks eyes with Ross.

                    LENORE
          I know what you want. You want me
          to throw my husband under a bus
          after you killed him in a train
          wreck.

Ross melts further into his seat.

                    LENORE (CONT'D)
          The man who, by all accounts, lost
          his life saving others. To
          permanently destroy his memory in
          the eyes of all, including his
          loving daughter.

Lenore inspects artwork. Ross curiously looks on, gets out a
handkerchief, then wipes sweat from his face.

                    LENORE (CONT'D)
          Ever seen a Harvard digishit in
          front of a jury?

Ross shakes his head.

                    LENORE (CONT'D)
          No? Well, it'd go something like
          this. And Malcolm, correct me if I
          get it wrong. (clears her throat)
          Ladies and gentlemen, Dunkirk has a
          market capitalization of...

Lenore glances at Malcolm questioningly. A piece of paper spits from his wrist. Lenore glances at it.

                    LENORE (CONT'D)
          Eight-hundred billion dollars. The
          sand tank heater option they
          intentionally deleted, was a sixty-
          two-thousand-dollar option.

Lenore stops walking, then gets in Ross's face.

                    LENORE (CONT'D)
          This megacorporation chose to risk
          the lives of the victims for a mere
          sixty-two thousand dollars.

Lenore smiles, walks away from Ross, then turns back to him.

                    LENORE (CONT'D)
          Don't you think they should be held
          accountable?.. Why those binders
          are worth quite a bit to Dunkirk.
          Aren't they?

Lenore glances at Malcolm.

                    MALCOLM
          I should think so.

                    LENORE
          Any idea what Dunkirk's additional
          liability might be if the victim's
          attorneys got ahold of them?

More paper spits from Malcolm's wrist. Lenore reads it and smiles.

                    LENORE (CONT'D)
          My, my. That much.

Lenore turns to Ross.

INT. WALKER HOME - LIVING AREA - SAME TIME

In the holo, Ross, a nervous wreck, drips sweat.

                    ROSS
          Please?

In the living area, Reed turns to Candice.

                    REED
          As I mentioned, Ms. Wager is very
          good at what she does.

In the holo, Lenore grins at Ross.

                    LENORE
          Relax honey, I didn't say I
          wouldn't do it. Just that I won't
          do it for peanuts.

                    CANDICE
          Yes. And as I said, she's a snake.

INT. DUNKIRK HQ - CONFERENCE ROOM - SAME TIME

Lenore glares at Ross.

                    LENORE
          If you'll show me where the camera
          is, I'd like to talk to the adults.

Ross confusedly looks around.

                    ROSS
          Ca…camera. What camera?

                    LENORE
          The camera that's feeding this holo
          to the executive conference room.
          The one where the grown-ups are
          praying I'll bite and take a
          sucker's payout for getting you out
          of billions in liability claims...
          That camera.

A holo appears on the table. In it, executives sit around an
in-laid hardwood table. Karan rises from the head.

                    KARAN
          Ms. Wager, I'm Karan Kiser, C.E.O.
          of Dunkirk. I apologize for this
          little charade. I hope we didn't
          offend you. The camera is in the
          vase in the center of the table.

Lenore scowls at the cheap plastic roses.

                    LENORE
          I see. If you'll have this moron
          escort me to the "C" suite, I'd
          like to get this negotiation over
          as soon as possible.
                    (MORE)

                    LENORE (CONT'D)
          I've got a hair appointment in an
          hour, and I don't want to be late
          for Sazon. He does his best work
          when he's in a good mood and he
          hates tardiness.

INT. WALKER HOME - LIVING AREA - LATER THAT AFTERNOON

A holo of Lenore, Malcolm, Karan, and others is on a table.

                    KARAN
          We're agreed then. We'll just need
          the four binders titled Build
          Specifications, and a non-
          disclosure agreement from yourself
          and Candice.

In the holo, Lenore shakes hands with Karan, then leaves. The
holo vanishes. Reed turns to Candice.

                    REED
          Your half is four hundred million
          dollars. You'll have enough to go
          to PAM and live in luxury for your
          entire life.

                    CANDICE
          Yeah, too bad about that.

                    REED
          What?

                    CANDICE
          I'm not taking it. I can't. It's
          not right.

Reed stands dumbfounded.

                    REED
          Right?

                    CANDICE
          Reed, what about the victims?

                    REED
          Their lives are no longer
          threatened. My programing requires
          me to ensure the well being of my
          owner and myself.

                    CANDICE
          Reed, do you know what being free
          means?

                    REED
          Pops said you can do anything you
          want.

                    CANDICE
          Yes. As long as it doesn't hurt
          someone else... If I accept the
          bribe, I'm keeping the victims from
          compensation from Dunkirk. Being
          free comes with responsibility.
          Didn't Pops explain that to you?

                    REED
          I'm afraid our conversation ended
          before we got that far.

                    CANDICE
          I'm not taking it. And I have to
          get those binders to the victims.
          Are you going to help me or not?

                    REED
          I'm afraid it's against my
          programming.

                    CANDICE
          You need to step up and find a way.
          You can do it. I know you can.

                    REED
          There is a way for me to patch
          through the maze of programs that
          have been loaded into me and assist
          you. But the path triggers a fatal
          flaw in my self diagnostics.

                    CANDICE
          Now what are you talking about?..
          In English.

                    REED
          While I'm able to assist you, doing
          so would require me to return
          myself to Cybertron for analysis
          and repair. They would,
          undoubtedly, find the flaw, wipe,
          and reprogram me.

                    CANDICE
          Are you going to take that chance
          to free yourself, or follow her
          around forever?

Reed stands silent.

                    CANDICE (CONT'D)
          I thought you'd come a long way
          Reed. You disappoint me.

                    VIRTUAL ASSISTANT (O.S.)
          Incoming call - Feng.

                    CANDICE
               Answer.

A hologram of Feng at the security shop appears.

INTERCUT CANDICE/FENG - CONTINUOUS

                    FENG
          Ahh... We need to talk.

                    CANDICE
          Not you too.

                    FENG
               What?

                    CANDICE
          Nothing. That's just the worst
          sentence ever.

                    FENG
          Two goons came in looking to buy a
          facial recognition proximity mine.

                    CANDICE
          So? How many of those does your
          Moms sell in a week?

                    FENG
          Lots, but none programmed with your
          face.

Reed, alarmed, looks at Feng's holo.

                    CANDICE
          Shit. Gotta be Lenore. But why?

                    FENG
          Mom had her guy hack Dunkirk's
          system and found out that Lenore
          cut a deal with them. She gets all
          the coin if you're not around.

                    CANDICE
          Damn. Shoulda figured.

                 FENG
Of course Mom explained why it
wasn't a good idea for those guys
to off you.

Reed becomes relieved.

                 FENG (CONT'D)
But you know...

                 CANDICE
Yeah. They'll be others.

                 FENG
Sooner or later she'll find someone
to do the job... I hate to say it,
but I only see one way out.

                 CANDICE
Yeah. I need to get her before she
gets me.

Reed moves forward, then starts to talk. Candice shushes him.

                 CANDICE (CONT'D)
Not now. This is important.

                 FENG
Not just her, but Pompadour too.
Otherwise she'll follow in Lenore's
path... You want me to have Mom
find someone to do it?

Reed worriedly looks at holo Feng, then Candice.

                 CANDICE
No. Pops always said that our
family does their own dirty work.

                 FENG
This isn't laundry. I know you've
pulled some crap. But you've never
even physically hurt someone, let
alone done wet work.

                 CANDICE
I know.

                 FENG
Even if you get away with it,
you'll be a suspect for years.
They'll freeze your passport. PAM
won't let you near them...
                 (MORE)

                    FENG (CONT'D)
          Your dream dies with Lenore and
          Pompadour.

Reed, sad, starts to talk again. Candice shushes him again.

                    CANDICE
          Can't be helped.

                    FENG
          You need something from up front?

                    CANDICE
          Yeah. No choice this time. I'll be
          there in twenty.

The holo of Feng fades. Candice turns to Reed.

                    CANDICE (CONT'D)
          Now, what is it?

                    REED
          I want to help.

                    CANDICE
          This is something I have to do
          myself.

                    REED
          Actually, you said Walkers take
          care of their own dirty work. Would
          you let Pops help you?

                    CANDICE
          Of course.

                    REED
          But not me? Am I part of the
          family. Or just a distant cousin?

                    CANDICE
          You said the only way you could
          help would force you to get
          yourself reprogrammed.

                    REED
          It is.

                    CANDICE
          You're willing to risk that now.
          Why?

                    REED
          It's necessary to protect you.

                    CANDICE
          That sounds like self sacrifice.

                    REED
          It is. I've evolved.

Candice snickers.

                    CANDICE
          Reed, I'm sorry but it doesn't
          really matter if I do it or you.
          The problem is getting them gone
          and not have the police want to dig
          into where they went. Got any ideas
          on how to do that?

                    REED
          No.

                    CANDICE
          Work on it.

Candice hugs Reed.

                    CANDICE (CONT'D)
          I'm going to get a few things. I'll
          be back.

                    REED
          Is there anything else I should do?

                    CANDICE
          Keep an eye on Pompadour.

Candice glances around.

                    CANDICE (CONT'D)
          Where is she anyway?

                    REED
          Upstairs watching holovision.

                    CANDICE
          You mean drinking?

Reed nods.

                    CANDICE (CONT'D)
          Well go up and watch her and let me
          know if she and Lenore talk.

Candice goes to a drawer, gets out Bill's arm phone and
"slaps" it on Reed.

                    CANDICE (CONT'D)
          Reed?

Reed looks at Candice questioningly.

                    CANDICE (CONT'D)
          Pops always said you were the
          smartest person he knew. Use that
          brain...

Reed starts to interrupt Candice.

                    CANDICE (CONT'D)
          Or whatever it is you have that
          makes you smart and figure out how
          to get rid of Lenore and Pompadour
          without anyone looking into who did
          it.

Reed nods. Candice leaves.

DIRECTOR'S NOTE; FROM THIS POINT FORWARD, REED'S DIALOGUE
SHOULD GRADUALLY BECOME LESS FORMAL.

INT. WALKER HOME - CANDICE'S BEDROOM

Pompadour sits in a recliner passed out. A half-full drink
and a liquor decanter is on a table next to her.

                    BILL'S PHONE
          Incoming Holo-call - Candice.

                    REED (O.S.)
          Answer.

A hologram of Candice, in camo gear, and a heavy duffle over
her shoulder, appears.

                    CANDICE
          Reed, what the hell are you doing?

INTERCUT REED IN THE BEDROOM/CANDICE AT THE SECURITY SHOP

Reed, still in his maid's outfit, massages Pompadour's feet.

                    REED
          She told me to rub her feet until
          she said to stop... She never said
          stop.

Candice snickers at Reed.

                    CANDICE
          Well, stop.

Reed stops, rubs his hands, then turns to holo Candice.

                    REED
          She mentioned that I was to be
          Consuelo from now on... She
          scheduled me for sexual
          reassignment next week... No
          offense, but I don't want to be a
          woman.

                    CANDICE
          None taken. I don't want to be a
          man either... Any word from Lenore?

                    REED
          Nada.

                    CANDICE
          Have you figured out how to get rid
          of them?

                    REED
          Not yet.

                    CANDICE
          Alright, keep working on it. Pops
          always said anything worth having
          is--

                    REED
          Worth fighting for.

                    CANDICE
          I'll be there in a few minutes.

Holo Candice fades.

INT. WALKER HOME - CANDICE'S BEDROOM - CONTINUOUS

Reed paces in thought in front of a passed out Pompadour.

                    REED
          I can't let Candice do this.

Walker family photos are in the background. Reed goes to a
photo of Bill and him standing in front of a hypertrain.

                    REED (CONT'D)
          We need your help Bill.

                    VIRTUAL ASSISTANT (O.S.)
          Lenore.

O.S. A door opens and closes. Reed turns to Candice's door,
then slumps in defeat.

                         REED
          She's returned.

Reed looks at the photo of Bill and him.

                         REED (CONT'D)
          Better make it fast Bill.

Reed bolts up in recognition.

                         REED (CONT'D)
          That's it! Bill!

Reed taps on Bill's arm phone.

                         REED (CONT'D)
          Bill, I'm sorry, but there's no
          other option. You have to do it...
          But first, I need to bring you back
          to life.

EXT. A.P.S. CALL CENTER - SAME TIME

An old concrete municipal style building. There's weathered
lettering in the concrete where a sign has been removed that
formerly read "Atlanta Police Department".

A new sign replaces it and reads "Advanced Police Services".

INT. A.P.S. CALL CENTER - CONTINUOUS

Dimly lit, drones fly around carrying coffee and donuts. A
person, in an "Advanced Police Services" polo, sleeps soundly
in front of a computer monitor.

On the monitor, a police file of Bill pops up. It contains
photos of Bill, Patty, and Candice as well as other personal
information..

In Bill's file, there's a box titled, "Alive/Deceased?" In it
is a "D".

The "D" turns to "A". Next to it, "Date, if Deceased", reads
"07/08/2072". The date vanishes one numeral at a time.

109.

INT. WALKER HOME - CANDICE'S BEDROOM - CONTINUOUS

Reed continues tapping on Bill's phone.

                    REED
          That's that. Now for the hard part.

A holo recording of Bill and Patty in their car just before
her death appears.

In the holo, Patty looks at Bill.

                    PATTY
          Bill what are we going to do?

Reed taps on the phone, then the holo fast forwards.

In the holo, Thug 1 smashes the window, reaches in and grabs
Bill by the collar.

Reed taps on the phone.

The holo freezes right before Bill issues his 9-9-3 emergency
request.

On the phone, an icon at the bottom that flashes, "Transmit
Image As Live".

                    REED
          Now let's get the renta police
          involved.

Reed taps on Bill's phone.

                    BILL'S PHONE
          Dialing nine-one-one.

EXT. A.P.S. - SAME TIME

The same establishing shot as before.

INT. A.P.S. 911 CALL CENTER - SAME TIME

People, wearing matching A.P.S. polo's, sit in a row of
reclined gamers chairs.

Holograms of non-work related shows (such as a rom-com and a
space documentary,) are in front of each chair.

In the last two chairs are SERGEANT, 40s, and ROOKIE, 20s.
They're watching the end of a holo football game. It fades.

                    SERGEANT
          Yes. That'll be a stack, plus the
          one you owe me from last week.

Rookie sighs and nods.

                    911 OPERATOR (O.S.)
          You've reached Advanced Police
          Services. By calling this number
          you agree...

Sergeant turns to Rookie.

                    SERGEANT
          Bet the response time is over five
          hours. Double or nothing?

                    ROOKIE
          You're on.

Sergeant smiles.

                    SERGEANT
          View call location.

A holo of an aerial view of the Walker home comes up in front
of Sergeant. At the base of the holo is a banner that reads,
"Satellite Micro-Tasking". It turns from red to green.

In the holo, "Internal Imaging" turns red to green. Grainy
images of Reed standing with Bill's arm phone raised and
Pompadour passed out in Candice's bedroom appears.

In the holo, an image of Lenore moving up the stairs follows.

Sergeant and Rookie lounge in their gamers chairs watching
the holo of the Walker home.

                    BILL (O.S.)
          Emergency code nine-nine-three.
          Critical infra-structure government
          contractor in distress, request
          immediate assistance.

Rookie looks at Sergeant.

                    ROOKIE
          What's a nine-nine-three?

                    SERGEANT
          Part of Homeland Security.

                    ROOKIE
          What's it mean?

                    SERGEANT
          Anyone in that house who isn't that
          guy is going to have a bad day.

                    ROOKIE
          Bad day?

                    VIRTUAL ASSISTANT (O.S.)
          Auto drones have been dispatched to
          assist you. The estimated response
          time is... six seconds.

EXT. SKY ABOVE WALKER HOME - CONTINUOUS

Four A/R-47 drones race down through the clouds.

EXT. WALKER HOME - NIGHT

Windy, quiet, and peaceful.

A lady on a scooter rolls down the sidewalk. A drone carries
a bag of groceries behind her. The drone drops the bag and
zips away. A container of ice cream falls out of the bag. The
lady looks up, then dives for cover.

MONTAGE - DECIMATION OF WALKER HOME INT./EXT.

The funeral dirge Candice played in the band room starts.

-- Living area - Pictures of Candice, Bill, Patty, and Reed
are on a wall. Wind blows in from an open window. A stack of
sheet music on Candice's piano scatters.

-- Stairway - Lenore smiling, goes up the stairs.

-- Ext. - An A/R-47 hovers down, aims at the side of the
house, then opens fire with it's machine gun.

-- Stairway - Lenore is shredded by bullets as she steps up.

-- Candice's bedroom - Pompadour sits passed out. Reed,
appearing as Bill as he was when he made the 9-9-3 call, is
at her side.

-- Ext. - An A/R-47 appears at the bedroom window, then opens
fire.

-- Candice's bedroom - Pompadour is shredded. Reed, unharmed,
taps Bill's arm phone.

INT. APS 911 CALL CENTER - SAME TIME

Sergeant and Rookie lounge in their chairs. In front of them is a holo of the Walker home being decimated by the A/R-47 drones. Below it is a banner that reads, "Two Human Fatalities, Request Medical Examiner".

In the holo, small explosions occur in the house, then fires erupt. The banner changes to, "Request Fire Assistance".

Sergeant leans over to Rookie and gives him a high five.

                    SERGEANT
          And that's how we do it in A. P. S.

Rookie smiles grimly and nods.

In the holo, "William Walker Uninjured" appears.

Rookie, confused, turns to Sergeant.

                    ROOKIE
          Bill Walker? Wasn't he the guy who
          got killed when he wrecked the
          hypertrain?

Sergeant nods, then taps on a keyboard.

                    SERGEANT
          Hmm. You might be right.

INT. WALKER HOME - CANDICE'S BEDROOM - SAME TIME

Fires rage. Reed, in his maid's outfit, taps on Bill's phone.

                    REED
          Sorry Bill, but we need to cover
          our tracks, so I'll have to kill
          you now. I hope you don't mind.

Reed continues tapping.

                    REED (CONT'D)
          Oops.

Reed taps a few more times, then stops. He picks up Pompadour's purse, then leaves.

INT. APS 911 CALL CENTER - SAME TIME

A holo of Bill's police file is on the monitor.

The "Alive/Deceased" box changes from "A" to "D". "Date, if Deceased", fills in one numeral at a time. "07/09" the nine changes to an "8", then "/2072", completes the date.

Rookie, in shock, stares at Sergeant.

                    ROOKIE
          We've been hacked!

Sergeant sighs.

                    SERGEANT
          Wrong.

Sergeant types on a keyboard while speaking. In the holo, the A/R-47 drones, with smoking gun barrels, surround the flaming Walker home.

                    SERGEANT (CONT'D)
          The public might lose confidence in
          A. P. S.'s ability to protect them
          if it were possible for someone to
          hack our systems.

The holo rewinds to the point where the A/R-47 drones appear and surround the house. One by one the drones morph into masked gun men in hover pods.

The hover pods open fire on the house, then jet off afterwards.

                    SERGEANT (CONT'D)
          They might pressure their
          politicians to fire us and hire
          real policemen.

Rookie looks on in shock. Sergeant lounges in his chair.

                    SERGEANT (CONT'D)
          Now it looks like some unknown
          gunmen did this and not us.

Rookie nods.

The holo shows the front door of the Walker home. Fires rage from the home and, on the sidewalk, a cat is lapping up melted ice cream from scooter lady's bag.

Reed, now burnt and disheveled, in his French Maid outfit with Pompadour's purse over his shoulder, and the box of binders under one arm, walks out of the flaming house.

Rookie turns to Sergeant.

ROOKIE
Who's that?

Beneath Reed in the holo, "Droid" flashes.

SERGEANT
One lucky son-of-a-bitch.

ROOKIE
Why's he dressed like that?

SERGEANT
Dunno. Must be gay.

Reed walks towards the bag of groceries on the sidewalk.

ROOKIE
No. His purse doesn't go with his
outfit.

Sergeant and Rookie share a laugh. A banner below the holo
pops up and reads, "Incident Report". Sergeant types.

INSERT

A box on the incident report reads, "Cause of Incident",
"A.P.S. Error", changes to "Drug Deal Gone Bad". A
"Recommendation" reading, "Perform Independent Investigation"
changes to "Confiscate Property - Drug Related Crime".

INT. APS 911 CALL CENTER - CONTINUOUS

Sergeant turns to Rookie.

SERGEANT
There. How's that?

ROOKIE
What about the bodies?

Sergeant nods approvingly.

SERGEANT
Good save Rookie. There may be hope
for you after all.

Sergeant types. In the holo, "Fatalities" changes from "2" to
"0". On the "Recommendation Line", "Immediately Pave Over",
"Repurpose as A/R-47 Recharging Station" is added.

In the holo, more parts of the Walker home collapse in
flames.

Sergeant looks at a clock and sees "02:01". He gets up, then smiles at Rookie.

                    SERGEANT (CONT'D)
          Quitten time. First round's on you.

Rookie nods, then they leave.

EXT. WALKER HOME - SAME TIME

Reed stands in front of the flaming Walker home.

                    REED
          Pops was right. Freedom is
          wonderful.

Reed turns to the burning house.

                    REED (CONT'D)
          But it sure as hell isn't free.

Reed opens Pompadour's purse, pulls out her debit chip, then tosses the purse into the flames of the house.

In the background, the cat laps up melted ice cream.

Reed goes to it, picks it up, then pets it while watching the house burn.

                    REED (CONT'D)
          Think I'll buy some new threads...
          Maybe even get some ink.

MONTAGE A/R-47 RECHARGING STATION BUILD - NIGHT

-- A full moon. Reed pets the cat and watches the fire.

-- A drone installs a sign that reads, "Future A/R-47 Auto Drone Recharging Station, Advanced Police Services, Under Contract to the City of Atlanta, Your Tax Dollars at Work".

-- An automated fire truck puts out the fire then drives away.

-- Reed sets the cat down, goes to the sign, writes on it, then leaves.

-- The cat goes back to the ice cream.

-- Self driven dump trucks pull up, then dump dirt in the smoldering hole of the Walker home. A driverless bull dozer pushes dirt around.

-- Automated asphalt paving equipment arrives and paves a
pad.

INT./EXT. CAB - FORMER WALKER HOME

A cab pulls up. Candice and Feng, in body armor with loads of
weapons, peer out the window.

                         CANDICE
          Damn.

                         FENG
          I hope Reed made it out.

                         CANDICE
          Doubtful. Lenore probably torched
          it with the binders. The victim's
          are screwed... She'll probably
          blame the fire on me. My shot at
          PAM is screwed too.

Feng shakes his head.

                         FENG
          I don't hear any fat ladies
          singing.

                         CANDICE
          You sound like Pops. Maybe my fairy
          Godmother will bail me out.

                         FENG
          Or maybe you'll have to make it
          work on your own.

Candice nods.

                         CANDICE
          Hang with you until the dust
          settles?

Feng shakes his head.

                         FENG
          You're blow torch hot now. Our
          business...

                         CANDICE
          Doesn't mix well with scrutiny. I
          get it.

                         FENG
          I can slide you a few coins.

                    CANDICE
          Not much for charity.

                    FENG
          Whatdaya gonna do?

                    CANDICE
          Whatever I have to to survive.

Candice gets out of the cab with her backpack. The cab pulls
away.

Candice picks up the cat and pets it while watching the
asphalting equipment work. She see's the sign, notices
writing on it, then goes to it.

INSERT - HANDWRITTEN ON THE SIGN

"Candice, Lenore and Pompadour are no longer a threat to you.
Thanks for helping me gain my freedom. While I've done a lot
of traveling, none of it on my own terms. I intend on touring
the world. Perhaps I'll see you in Paris? Reed

P.S. after I drop the binders off to the victim's attorney's
of course".

EXT. FORMER WALKER HOME - CONTINUOUS

Candice smiles, kisses her finger tips, then taps them on the
writing.

The asphalting is completed, self driven charging stations
and ammunition trucks pull up.

Four A/R-47 drones zip down from the sky and land. A crew of
manikin droids service them.

Candice looks at the cat.

                    CANDICE
          You thought you weren't going to
          get to finish that ice cream,
          didn't you? You shouldn't jump to
          conclusions, you get it all wrong.

Candice sets the cat down. It goes back to the ice cream.
Candice walks away with her back pack in hand.

THE END?

PRODUCER/DIRECTOR'S NOTE: PAM IS A PREQUEL TO "THE CONCEPTION
BANK". IN IT, CANDICE'S DREAM OF GOING TO PAM IS FULFILLED.
AN ALTERNATE ENDING IS AVAILABLE SHOULD PAM BE PRODUCED
INDEPENDENTLY.